Unbalanced

No Rival #4

Charity Parkerson

Punk & Sissy Publications
--Warning: This book is intended for readers over the age of 18.

Copyright © 2016 Charity Parkerson
Editor: Vicky Reese
ISBN-10:1-946099-04-X
ISBN-13:978-1-946099-04-4
Note: This book was originally published under the same title
with Ellora's Cave Publishing.

Using unmatched skill and intelligence, Kurt captures the attention of every partner he desires. His ability to confuse his prey keeps them captivated. This trick has never failed him. That is, until he meets McKenna.

Author McKenna Jones has gone to great lengths to ensure the details of her erotic books are airtight. When Kurt challenges one of her scenes, she doesn't hesitate to take up his offer to prove his theory. The bad boy MMA fighter appeals to her on every level. Kurt's intelligence stimulates her mind even as his touch sets her body on fire. Although McKenna would rather not add her name to his list of ex-lovers, she cannot resist his pull.

McKenna's odd behavior exasperates Kurt. She is an addiction he cannot shake, but somehow the two of them need to make the combination of his OCD logic and her unbalanced nature work, because a surprise is about to turn their lives upside down.

Dedication

For every department store clerk who didn't call me crazy—to my face—as I sniffed each business suit and men's cologne I came across while writing this book. You earned your angel wings.

Chapter One

November

She wasn't wearing shoes. Funnily enough, it was the first detail about her that caught his eye. At a table, in public, Kurt found her shoeless state odd. There were a thousand tiny things about her he should have noticed first. Without a doubt, her plain black t-shirt, yoga pants, and the overall lack of effort toward her appearance allowed her to blend into the background. It shouldn't have mattered. Kurt wasn't usually so blind. None of those points stole an ounce of power from her beauty. There wasn't a hint of makeup marring her face. Blonde curls piled on her head, held in place by some sort of clip. Something about her eyes held him captivated. They were unfocused as they moved across the pages of the book she held between her hands. In spite of that, he felt sure she absorbed every word, only on a different plane than others would.

He moved closer. The lack of footwear became an obsession. Curiosity ate at him. He needed to know why. The coffee shop located inside a G. Richards' Bookstore had a sign posted clearly on the front door. "No shoes. No service." Once Kurt managed to snag the chair directly across from her, he bent at the waist. Under the guise of dropping a napkin, he peered under the edge of her table. Suspicions confirmed. His brows drew together in a frown as he sat up.

After a moment of staring at the corner, he couldn't stand it any longer. "Your feet are bare."

Lifting her gaze from the book between her hands, she blinked several times. He could practically see her dragging her mind away from whatever cloud it was on.

"What?"

"Your feet," he repeated. "They have no shoes on them."

"Oh. I'd forgotten." She immediately dismissed him by returning to her reading.

"You're inside a business. They serve food."

She didn't bother glancing his way as she responded. "If that bothers you, I won't mention the state of my underwear."

He had to know. "Did you forget those, as well?"

That got her attention. A line formed between her eyes as if his question was too stupid for her to fathom.

"How does someone forget their underwear?"

"How does a person forget their

8

shoes?" he shot back.

Tilting her head to one side, she seemed to think it over for a moment before responding. "Is this a trick question?"

Kurt scoffed as he reminded her of the obvious. "You're not wearing them."

Her mouth turned up in one corner in such a way his gaze immediately shot to her lips. "I'm aware."

Unable to keep the exasperation from his voice, Kurt sighed. "You said you'd forgotten your shoes. It stands to reason, then, you would know how one goes about it."

Setting her book aside, she nodded slowly as if giving his theory due consideration. "Your logic is sound," she admitted after a moment. Finally, they were getting somewhere. She immediately ruined it by adding, "Except, I said no such thing. Therefore, I cannot help you."

There was a moment where he had nothing. He couldn't recall a single incident where anyone had caused his mind to go blank. His brain was always on the move, slightly dissatisfied with his lot. She'd wiped him clean. Her blue eyes focused on him fully as if awaiting his next move. When he wasn't quick enough, she released a heavy sigh.

"If you must know, when I got here I realized I had on two different-colored shoes so I took them off."

Without waiting to see his reaction, she flipped her book up between them, shutting him out. A part of him wanted to laugh at her confession. He was too fascinated. Not to mention, with his curiosity assuaged he really wanted to hear more about the rest.

"What about your underwear?"

She ignored him. He bit back a smile. His mind whirled back to life and he searched for a new way to insert himself into her company. Tilting his head, he read the title blocking her eyes from his gaze. *The Ins and Outs of BDSM.* Catchy title. Switching his gaze to the other items scattered across her table, he took note of another book on bondage as well as some handwritten notes. As far as he could tell by what she'd scratched out, she was either intent on rocking some dude's world or plotting one hell of a murder.

He braced his elbows on the table, lowering his voice to where only she could hear. "I have handcuffs back at my place."

She set the book aside. Mimicking his pose, her eyes shone with mirth as she pitched her voice low, as well. "I have a Taser in my handbag."

Holding back his laughter, Kurt

didn't miss a beat. "Kinky," he said, adding a wink. "I like it."

Snorting, she slapped her hand over her mouth and nose as if she couldn't believe what she'd done.

"I'm Kurt," he offered before she could escape into her mind again.

"McKenna."

*

He had handcuffs. She bet he did. The only statement Kurt had made that McKenna found surprising was that they were back at his place. The in-your-face piercings, tattoos, and biker boots look had her expecting him to whip them out right then and slam them down on the table between them. Why did she attract all the weirdoes? She was the weirdo whisperer. They found her everywhere she went. Of course, she was the real dumbass in the equation because she'd given him her name.

"Are you studying to become a Madam?"

"Where are you from?" It wasn't an attempt to block on McKenna's part. She really didn't want to talk about her work with a stranger but he had an odd accent. Perhaps it was more that he didn't have an accent at all, yet he spoke as if English was not his first language.

"Here and there."

He was wasting her time. She didn't like time stealers.

"I have things to do." The words popped out. It happened more often than she liked. Still, she didn't know him. Why should she be thrust into polite conversation? Deciding she shouldn't, McKenna pulled her notebook closer. She didn't know where her pen had gone.

"Are you looking for this?" A

triumphant smile lit his face as she spotted her pen between his fingers. He turned it over in his hands and peered closer at it. "Hmm, McKenna Jones, Best Selling Author. Interesting. Am I to assume you're the McKenna Jones on this pen?"

An inner groan sounded loud inside her head. She wanted to kick her own ass. The pens were meant for fans but nine times out of ten, she ended up keeping them for herself. She went through a lot of ink. Of course, it had never occurred to her they would lead a psycho to her door.

This time she was blocking. "How am I supposed to be responsible for what you assume? You are a grown man."

His eyes hooded at her words. Damn. Hadn't being an erotica author taught her anything? It was hard work weighing her every response to make sure it couldn't be misconstrued once it left her mouth.

"You haven't seen the whole package...yet. I'm still capable of growing a bit more."

She could stab him in the eye. Well, probably she couldn't, but she could make him her bitch in her next book.

His eyes lit with challenge. "How do you intend to make me your bitch?"

Oh dear. She really needed to pay closer to what her mouth was doing while her mind was otherwise engaged. "I have no idea what you're talking about."

His lips parted as if she'd shocked him speechless with her blatant lie. Lying was her job. Why were people surprised by it? He made an obvious attempt to recover.

"You just..." he paused and a new light entered his green eyes. "Oh. I see. You're crazy."

15

Ouch. McKenna dropped her gaze to the notebook, shutting him out. This was why she didn't like people. They didn't understand. A word she'd written earlier caught her attention. Everything else disappeared. She needed to google fetishes. These books weren't helping. There wasn't a single reference to any of the unique fetishes people had. She really wanted Luke to have some freaky thing he enjoyed doing in the bedroom. Of course, it couldn't be anything too strange or she wouldn't be able to help Lacey fall in love with him. Damn. Sometimes it was hard making characters do what she wanted. Every time she thought she had the storyline figured out, one of them would end up falling for a side character instead. This damn deadline was staring her in the face. Everyone wanted the sexy fireman to end up with Lacey. Neither of her stubborn characters wanted to listen to her.

McKenna was halfway through packing up her belongings before she realized Kurt was gone. An unexpected pang hit her in the chest. It was stupid. Her mind was crowded with fictional characters who wouldn't quit talking long enough for her to have any peace. Sliding her notebook closer, she moved to flip it closed but at the last second, she spotted two words written on the page in someone else's handwriting.

"I'm sorry."

The twinge hit her again. Reaching up she rubbed the spot in her chest that was aching. It was ridiculous she should be so lonely when she was never alone. The words blurred and McKenna blinked back tears. The bastard had stolen her pen.

He'd called her crazy...him. As if he had any fucking right. Fuck. This was why he stayed on his own playground. There were no misunderstandings. All the participants here did more than recognize their demons. They embraced them.

The darkened alcove outside club Affinity was perfect for a little late-night action. Working security at the door got boring otherwise. People didn't flood the exclusive fetish club all at once. There was never a line built up outside the door. They trickled in a few at a time, with sneaking glances and under the cover of darkness. This gave Kurt time to inspect the wares. He enjoyed measuring each new prospect, weighing their gumption. Most of all, Kurt loved finding people's boundaries and pushing them over. He wasn't picky in the traditional sense. Body type, gender or certain coloration didn't factor into his decision at all. It ran deeper. A strong sense of self-worth tasted smoother than the finest whiskey going down.

Tonight was no exception. The caramel-skinned male—whose ass was currently cradled against Kurt's hips—didn't prefer men. Kurt wasn't any man though and once he set his sights on someone, it was only a matter of time. Cupping Patrick's jaw, Kurt tilted his head back, holding it steady against his shoulder.

Speaking quietly against his ear, Kurt wooed him with the pitch of his voice. "Is this what you've been missing?" he asked as he slid his other hand down the front of Patrick's body.

The button and zipper of the man's jeans easily gave way beneath Kurt's fingers. The sound of Patrick's labored breaths kicked up a notch. Counting slowly to three in his head, Kurt intentionally drew out the anticipation before encircling Patrick's erection. His reward came when the man released a heartfelt moan.

"I'm what you've been lacking," Kurt assured him with a stroke of the smooth skin beneath his fingertips. He brushed the silver ring on his thumb over the man's crown. The moisture seeping out told him more than the sounds Patrick made. "This is delicious when it hits the back of my throat. There're so many things I could do for you. Can you picture it? Close your eyes and imagine me on my knees."

Kurt didn't lift his gaze from his prize to see if Patrick obeyed. He knew he would. Handling Patrick's dick as he would his own, Kurt increased the steady speed of his pumping. "My cheeks are hollowed out as you slide down as deep as you can go. I'm tightened around you with wet heat lapping at your dick. You fuck my mouth the way you've been imagining for weeks."

The slight twitch in muscle spoke volumes about how close Patrick was to orgasm. At the last second, Kurt tightened his grip at the head of Patrick's cock, holding still and cutting off the man's release. An audibly strangled cry caught in Patrick's throat. He bucked against Kurt's hand as if seeking the pleasure he'd been denied. Touching his lips to his ear, Kurt soothed him with his voice. "I won't disappoint." He closed his mouth around Patrick's lobe, sucking lightly. "Damn, I wish this was your dick."

Patrick whimpered. Returning to a gentle stroke of his shaft, Kurt rotated his hips, grinding his erection against the man's ass. "Brace yourself," he warned. "You're about to learn what all the multiple-orgasm hype is about."

* * * * *

The street below his apartment was noisy as hell. He was used to it for the most part. There were nights, like tonight, when the sound of traffic competed for attention with all the thoughts running through his overactive brain. It was times such as these he thought he might go insane from the noise. It was already too late at night to go to the Warehouse District and sign up for a fight. An unsanctioned, no-holds-barred bout was exactly what he needed to rid himself of the extra energy. Instead, he plugged his guitar into its amp and the computer before attaching his headphones as well. The result was a muffled song only he could hear while his music program recorded the notes of the tune floating across his mind. If it weren't for the neighbors who'd been stuck with him, he wouldn't worry over the noise. There was no reason for everyone to pay due to his inability to settle down. Five chords in and he was still crawling out of his skin. He was incapable of escape.

Ripping off the headphones, Kurt paced the room, unable to find a single ounce of peace. He glanced at the clock. There wasn't a reason. It simply gave him something to do with his eyes. Things hadn't this bad in a long time. Reaching inside his back pocket, he pulled out McKenna's pen. Was he feeling guilty over the way he'd left things? He'd left a note. She may not have seen it or even more likely, she might feel his piss-poor apology wasn't good enough.

He flipped his laptop toward him

and did a quick Internet search for McKenna Jones. His hope was there would be an email address available for the public. He should make some attempt to set the matter right. The look on her face before she'd hidden it from view kept flashing through his mind. He scrubbed his hands through his hair. Yeah. He needed to offer a better apology. Sixty-seven pages of Google results popped up on the screen. Her website was listed first. He clicked on it. His eyes widened as the website opened. An amazingly sexy picture of McKenna wearing an all-leather outfit filled the screen. It was only supposed to be the background image. Kurt wasn't seeing anything else on the page. It was her. There wasn't a doubt in his mind. He had a photographic memory, especially when it came to beautiful objects. McKenna Jones was one of the rarest gems he'd ever seen. He'd called her crazy. Tearing his eyes away from her face, he checked out the list of books. They were erotica, which explained a great deal. Each book title contained something about the devil. *The Devil I Know. The Devil I Love. The Devil I Desire.* The list went on and on until there were twenty-five in total.

Of course, unlike her, he believed in modern-day reading. Pulling out the rolling chair from underneath the desk, he sat down at the computer. Following the book's link, he downloaded the first story in the series to his e-reader. In a matter of a few clicks, he owned his first McKenna Jones book. He read a few lines aloud, attempting to get a feel for her writing style.

"I first encountered the devil on All Hallows' Eve. The moment our gazes met,

I recognized his depravity. In a single glance he caused me to fear for my sanity, pray for my soul."

He settled deeper in his chair. "Oh. This would be good."

Chapter Two

Checking her email was always an adventure. One McKenna had learned was best done first thing in the morning while the coffee still flowed hot. The delicious smell of new books and lattes filled the air of the G. Richards' Bookstore. Claiming a table and Wi-Fi access in the overcrowded store was the easy part of her morning routine. In her usual one eye closed and cringing fashion, she logged on. It had been a few months since she'd received any video clips of men masturbating, but the damage was done. She was scarred for life. The first ten emails were ads for promotional materials. She had two requests for an interview on book blogger sites. Twitter managed, as usual, to fill her account with notifications from people who sent out those awful "welcome" direct messages. One day she'd remember to turn her email updates off for that site. Scanning the rest of her inbox, she spotted a contact form notification from her website. Those were her favorite.

"I promise I'm not a stalker. After arriving home, I decided a formal apology was in order. Here it is. I, Kurt Travis, do hereby withdrawal my earlier statement. You—most likely—are not crazy. Even if you are, you did nothing to deserve my rude behavior. Please accept my humblest apologies."

"I couldn't sleep last night."

McKenna blinked in surprise as the man who'd sent the message appeared across from her. She'd be damned if she'd let him see her shock.

"Is it because you're a pen thief? I've heard a guilty conscience can interrupt sleep patterns."

"No."

"I thought you weren't a stalker."

"Oh good. You got my email. I have a problem with your book."

"I have several books. You'll have to narrow it down."

"The first devil book," he answered as if it should have been obvious. "I read it last night. You should stick to writing what you know."

She worked at keeping her face blank. "I'd prefer a stalker. Admittedly, there's a chance I'd end up dead in their basement but—in all likelihood—they wouldn't insult me as often as you."

He merely blinked, as if she'd spoken a language he couldn't understand, before continuing, "Anyhow, it's obvious when you write emotion, it comes from the heart. Those bits are very good. Unfortunately, it's immediately obvious to anyone who has ever been tied to a bed that you have not."

She waited for more. Four hundred pages that he'd supposedly read in one night and he'd walked away with one thing.

When she didn't say anything, he added. "It's the little details." He stared at her as if everything should now be clear. Nope. She had nothing. He released a heavy sigh.

"Okay. On page 173, Celeste's hands were bound to the rungs of the bed with rope. Every other scene, up to this point and after this one, is done in great detail. I find it hard to believe you meant this bit to be an exception. Following my theory, it stands to reason you said exactly what you intended. Only masochists would allow themselves to be treated in such a way and Celeste didn't strike me as such. Even if someone chose to use rope, there would be either something wrapped around it or around the wrists to protect the skin from damage. Generally, a softer material is used in bondage."

"Wow." His smile was a bit too triumphant for her liking. "You remember the exact page number it was on."

"I have a photographic memory," he explained, waving off her statement. "Can I expect similar nonsense from the rest of the series?"

She shrugged and took a sip of her coffee before answering. "Only if you read it."

"Didn't I say as much?"

It seemed useless to point out he had not, in fact, said as much.

"I've decided you need my help."

She took another drink in an attempt to hold her smart assery on the inside before responding. "How so?" She almost high-fived herself for sounding so adult-like. Her big-girl panties were on and she'd not kicked him in the balls or anything.

"By offering to take you back to my place. I'll tie you up the right way, purely for scholarly purposes. You'll be completely safe and I swear I will not accost you in any manner. I love to read and you need better research before attempting this type of scene again."

McKenna closed her laptop and slid out of her seat. "Okay. Let's go."

His expression made her wonder if she'd grown a second head. "I didn't expect you to agree."

"Why? As you said, it's purely for scholarly pursuit. I've done a lot of crazy stuff in the name of research. Why should this be any different?" She headed for the door. "Oh. Hold on for a second." Changing directions, McKenna moved to the counter and handed her laptop to the girl working behind it. "Would you take care of this for me?"

Flipping her red hair over one shoulder, the woman relieved McKenna of her burden. "Of course." Flashing a grateful smile, McKenna moved back to Kurt's side.

"Okay. I'm ready."

He shot a glance over her shoulder before meeting her stare once more. "Did you just give your computer to a complete stranger?"

His question confused her. "Why would I do such a thing?"

Kurt shook his head. "I have no idea," he muttered after a second of gawking at her.

Really? The man acted as if she had

no sense. He was the one taking her home with him. For all he knew, she was a serial killer.

* * * * *

His apartment was like something out of a horror movie. His bookshelves were not only alphabetized, they were also separated by size. The bottles of cologne resting on his dresser were color coded and facing in the same direction. She was willing to bet money his canned goods all had their labels facing out. The final straw for McKenna was when she caught a glimpse of his shoes lined up perfectly at the end of his bed. Bending over, she pretended to inspect the titles on the shelf while intentionally rearranging the books.

"You have a wild variety of books. Most of these aren't in English."

"I speak seven languages." His explanation caused her to turn.

"I noticed you have an odd accent but when I asked where you're from yesterday, you never answered me."

He nodded but his eyes were locked on the bookcase. A frown appeared between his brows. "I was born in Russia where I lived in foster care until I turned eight when a German couple adopted me. The arrangement lasted two years before they abandoned me on the streets of France."

"They abandoned you? How awful!"

He shrugged. "Life is hard for everyone."

"What happened then?" McKenna asked. Moving to stand at the end of his bed, she waited until he wandered over to the shelves in an obvious attempt to decide what was wrong with them. The moment his back turned, she used her foot to scatter the perfectly aligned shoes, even going as far as to kick a few underneath the bed. It was for his own good. This level of organization wasn't healthy for anyone. Leaning over, she went even further by reaching beneath his comforter and pulling the sheet off the bed. Only on one corner so he wouldn't discover it until he went to bed.

"I lived on the streets," he answered, dragging her back on topic. "I learned to fight and survive. I moved around a lot. Eventually, I made my way here."

"That's a terrible story. Now would you like to tell me the truth?"

He threw his head back on a roar of laughter. The sound caught her by surprise. "What gave me away?"

"Only every single detail. I tell stories for a living. You had the same awkward tone to your voice as I do when I'm attempting to tell someone what my current work in progress is about."

Deciding he simply didn't want to tell her about his life, she took pity on him. Pointing at an electric guitar plugged into his computer. "Do you have a program keeping track of scoring your notes? I've heard of those before but I've never seen one in action."

For the first time since meeting him, Kurt looked uncomfortable. "Um. Yeah. Music is a bit of a hobby."

Plopping down on the bed, she waved in the direction of the guitar. "Would you show me how it works?"

His features shifted. It was instantaneous. A mask fell into place and McKenna found herself staring at a version of Kurt she didn't like. It was the one who enjoyed wasting her time. A wicked glint lit his eyes. His voice became sultry. "I have other things I could show you. You wouldn't regret it."

"If you're intent on introducing me to the world of perfectly pressed pants and color-coded sock drawers, I'll pass. On the other hand, if you meant your statement as a sexual reference, I feel moved to remind you I write erotica. I have no doubt you're skilled. Look at your apartment. If you put half the effort into satisfying your partner as you do in organizing your shit, then I imagine you could ruin a person. With all that said and my scatterbrain nature aside, I would rock your fucking world." She allowed her words to hang in the air between them, enjoying the sight of his shock for a moment before adding, "I don't like people who waste my time. If you're uncomfortable playing in front of an audience, say so. No one understands exposing their soul for public ridicule the way I do. Please be genuine or leave me alone. It's not necessary for me to leave my house to enjoy a bit of make-believe."

He leaned against the edge of the desk, eyeing her as if attempting to decide how determined she was. It was equally possible he was searching for a new way to manipulate her. She acknowledged the truth with an inner sigh.

"Fair enough," he agreed after a moment. "I'm from San Jose, California. Although I was raised in the States, my mother was German. My father, a Texan. It's almost impossible to avoid gaining a hint of accent when it's part of your upbringing, except the differences between the two intonations obviously left me confused. I ended up an odd cross between the pair. Not to mention, my ability to speak several languages fluently has influenced my pronunciation of English words. A year and a half before I was due to graduate from Stanford, my parents were killed in an accident while visiting family overseas. I dropped out and moved here."

It was partially true. She could hear it in his words. Unfortunately, she couldn't decide which parts were a lie. She let it go.

"And the music?"

"I'm not very good," he admitted dryly.

"Do you love it?" He gave her a short nod. "Then you will be," she assured him. She pushed backward on the bed until she could spread out and rest her head on his pillow. After lifting her arms above her head, she grabbed hold of one of the oak rungs of his headboard. McKenna awaited her fate. Unfortunately, even as his eyes darkened and he moved to give in to her silent demand, she couldn't remain quiet.

Her nervous habit of chattering kicked in.

"In some aspects we are very similar. We both have creative minds and both of my parents are gone, as well. Of course, there wasn't anything tragic behind their passing." She paused to think it over before adding, "Unless you consider the fact I am now alone in the world. They had me late in life and weren't in good health. Once my mother was gone, my father simply faded away shortly after."

McKenna assumed Kurt was listening. It was hard to tell since he didn't allow it to slow him down. In short order, some form of velvet material encircled her wrists. His chest hovered two inches from her face. All she needed to do was lift her head. She could flatten her tongue over the rings outlined against his tight t-shirt. He smelled like cinnamon. She really liked that particular spice. Her nipples hardened. Letting her breath out slowly, McKenna worked at breathing though her mouth instead. This man would eat her alive. Hadn't she learned her lesson yet? Men such as him decimated people like her, leaving them with nothing. The reminder gave her strength even as the binding tightened.

*

McKenna's scent filled his lungs. Even the fact she wore her shoes on his bed couldn't distract him. Her supple body caused his stomach to clench with hunger. The way she willingly submitted called to his wild nature. Her unquestioning trust wrecked him. He wouldn't let her down. With her hands bound, he ignored the pounding of his erection against the zipper of his jeans. Sitting at her side, he silently awaited her judgment. Her face screwed up in thought. Tugging the material, she curled her nose. It was adorable.

"This is unpleasant. I think I'll skip it in the future."

He huffed. It wasn't intentional. She wasn't getting the full experience. "You're missing the point. This is completely different when you're turned on. Arousal steals away the discomfort. Handing over control frees your mind to enjoy your partner's plans without plotting your next move. You're looking at this from a scholarly point of view. Bondage isn't one dimensional."

She gave up her struggle and met his gaze. "This isn't real control. It's the illusion of domination."

He was willing to debate. "I'm listening."

She rolled her eyes. "There are some

particulars you can't express in words. I need to demonstrate. Kiss me."

The demand almost caused him to fall off the bed. "Are you being serious?"

Her expression gave nothing away. "Yes. Kiss me." There wasn't a hint of heat in her tone. She was still in educational mode. It was unacceptable.

He'd like to think she didn't need to tell him twice except she already had. Refusing to miss his chance, he was determined to chuck every ounce of skill behind it. Throwing his leg over her body, he straddled her hips, pinning her in place. Leaning in, he paused a hair's breath away from her lips, hoping to build anticipation of his touch. She closed the distance. The moment their lips met, hers parted. Teeth sank lightly into his bottom lip before McKenna swiped her tongue over it, as if apologizing. He opened for her. She didn't hold back. The taste of coffee and some form of mint greeted his taste buds. The tip of her tongue stroked the roof of his mouth. He chased her. She probed the stud in his tongue. She'd known it was there he realized, even though he took great pains not to show it when he spoke. A moan rose in his throat. She was incredible. Every subtle move she made bespoke skill. Each brush of her lips, tongue and teeth went straight to his cock. He needed to possess her. More importantly, he wanted her hands free. Reaching up, he worked the knots at her wrists loose without breaking their kiss. If her mouth was this skilled, her hands had to be ten times as talented.

The moment she was free to do so, she pushed until he was on his back. Her hot center cradled his hard dick as she straddled his hips. She ran her fingers through his hair, deepening their kiss. Easing up, she held his bottom lip between hers. Her breath fanned across it. The tip of her tongue swiped it one final time before letting go. She hovered less than an inch away from his mouth.

"I told you to kiss me and you did because your idea of bondage is not control. I say this is an illusion because your velvet binding secured me with the promise of pleasure. A devil's domination would be tangible, with rope and a sure knowledge of pain if you disobeyed."

Realization slammed into him at her words. He'd been wrong. She had done this before. Even though this wasn't her first time, she'd still gone along with his plan. "I don't do anything without a purpose." With her taunt hanging between them, she pushed away. Moving across the room, McKenna picked up a stack of blank sticky notes from his desk.

"Can I use these?"

"Wouldn't you rather have paper?"

"No. These."

Her gaze was slightly unfocussed, her hair mussed. It was fucking sexy. His dick twitched. Realizing she was waiting for an answer, he cleared his throat. "Yeah. Go for it."

Even to him, Kurt sounded ravaged. As he looked on, she chose a pen from his desk before rejoining him on the bed. There was no way she was missing the line of his erection. He couldn't move. The fear of permanent injury kept him pinned in place. She settled in close enough that he could feel the heat of her body against his hip. With the notes balanced on her knee, McKenna bent over them and set to work. It was as if she disappeared. The change in the air was almost tangible. One moment her fire blasted his body and the next she turned inside herself, leaving the real world behind for her metaphysical planet.

Sucking in a deep breath, he sat up. In an attempt at calling his body under control, he put some distance between them. His mind stayed behind, lingering over their kiss even as his body wandered across the room. McKenna's disconnection felt so complete, Kurt picked up his guitar without thought. The notes floating across his brain flowed through the instrument. His laptop fired to life recording each one. Tiny details from their encounter became sharper as his mind cleared. There were too many factors. Her actions couldn't have been calculated. His fingers paused. The music fell silent. Rearranging the timing in his head, he started over. Following the path of every possible scenario, Kurt still couldn't decipher the logic behind her actions. She was simply fascinating.

It took Kurt a moment to realize, he'd been staring blankly at the wall without playing a single chord long enough so his computer screen had gone black. He glanced over his shoulder. Several lines of yellow sticky notes covered the wall above his headboard. On her side and facing him, McKenna slept silently with her head pillowed by her arms.

Setting the guitar aside, Kurt did his best not to wake her as he climbed onto the bed. The moment he settled in behind her, McKenna snuggled against his chest. Although he knew she was asleep and therefore not responsible for her actions, her words were still fresh on his mind. *I don't do anything without a purpose.* Why then had she kissed him? If he was being honest with himself, she'd not shown any real interest in him before the moment her lips met his.

Shifting positions, his foot hit a lump in the covers. He rolled onto his back. What the hell was wrong with his bedding? He ran his foot over the spot. Before he had a chance to inspect it further, McKenna rolled over and threw her leg over his waist. She used his chest as a pillow. The lump underneath the comforter was driving him insane. A low moan slipped from McKenna's lips. Fuck it. He didn't need to fix the covers. There was a hot woman in his arms. Not to mention, as hard as his dick was, there was no way in hell he would be able to sleep anyhow.

* * * * *

The bed shifted near his head. Kurt came awake with a start. Blinking in surprise, he stared up at the woman standing on the bed. She was straddling his head. With one foot firmly planted on either side of him, McKenna scribbled on the sticky notes on the wall. Between her leaning forward and his angle from below, he could see straight up her shirt. She was wearing a black lace bra. There was also a smallish tattoo on her ribs. He couldn't make out what it was. Still, the view was good. Incredible didn't begin to describe McKenna's body. With soft curves and breasts that would overflow in his hands, she was delicious. Kurt would've given anything to see inside her mind. He imagined thousands of flashes of brilliance firing all at once. Every single one of them led to the same place—sexual pleasure. Unable to stand another moment without touching her, he snagged her legs. In a move normally reserved for the cage, he flipped her off her feet and rolled her beneath him in one fluid motion. A high-pitched giggle rent the air.

Holding both her wrists high above her head with one hand, he pinned her lower body to the mattress by straddling her hips. Her blue eyes lit up. A flush covered her skin. His apartment had never seen happiness before. He wondered if it would catch fire even as he used his free hand to shove the hem of her shirt upward. McKenna's laughter died on a squeak. Determination drove him. He needed to know or he wouldn't be able to sleep again.

"What the—"

"It's a never-ending circle," he said cutting off her question as he exposed the tattoo. Tilting his head to the side, he read the words out loud. "While I was dreaming I lost." He studied it a moment longer.

Written in a perfect circle, only the person who wore a never-ending saying knew exactly which way it was meant to be read. "Or is it, I lost while I was dreaming?"

The happiness had left her eyes. "Does it matter?"

No. He didn't suppose it did. Either way, it meant the same thing. "What did you lose?"

She didn't answer. "I'll let you know what mine means if you tell me."

"Really?" In one word, McKenna sang the entire "liar, liar, pants on fire" song. Carefully, so he wouldn't squash her, Kurt sat back on his heels and pulled his shirt over his head. Her gaze locked on his chest. Ah, there was the lust she'd not shown before now. He watched as she absorbed the sight of his body. While he waited for her to notice what he intended her to see, he pondered over a possible permanent limp. She kept him hard. Sucking in a breath, he called on every ounce of self-control when McKenna traced the ridges in his abdomen. He knew the exact moment she finally spotted his endless circle tattoo. Her fingers froze. With the massive amount of markings on his torso, he'd known it would take her a minute to work it out.

"Trapped in a prison without bars," she read aloud. She met his gaze. "I'd love to be imprisoned inside your head. It's full of music, foreign languages, and blinding intellect. From here, it looks beautiful."

She left him speechless. There wasn't another person in the world like her. He was sure of it. A thousand confessions raced to the tip of his tongue. He wanted to tell her all about how his mind wasn't the least bit attractive. It was obsessive. His psyche didn't hold him prisoner. He purposely barred himself away while locking others out. Otherwise, he was too much of everything for anyone to handle. None of those details passed his lips. Instead, he asked again, "What did you lose?"

"Everything." Taking advantage of his shocked haze, she wiggled out of his hold. "I'm starving. Can you take me back to the bookstore?"

Her words snapped him out his thoughts. His gaze shot to the clock. Four p.m. He'd slept the whole day. When was the last time he'd slept more than three hours at one time? Kurt couldn't remember. It had been years. McKenna was standing by the door waiting.

"Give me a minute." After a quick trip to the bathroom, he yanked his shirt back on and grabbed a jacket. "What time does the bookstore close?"

McKenna followed him outside. "Six. Why?"

"Since I'm taking you to dinner, I need to know how much time I have."

An adorable frown touched her face as he opened the car door for her. "What does dinner have to do with the bookstore?"

"You left your laptop there," he reminded her.

"No. I didn't."

He was sure she had. He'd watched her do so but he didn't argue until he slid behind the wheel. It was too cold to stand outside debating the matter.

"Seriously?" he asked the moment his ass hit the seat. "I was standing right there when you handed it to the girl working behind the counter."

Her expression cleared. "You'll think this is crazy."

"I doubt it." He saw his death in her eyes. She crossed her arms over her chest, staring straight ahead. It took him a minute to realize she didn't intend to say more. "It was a joke, McKenna. I know you're not crazy."

"I don't expect you to lie to me to be my friend," she muttered, sounding the same as a petulant child. "I'd planned to say, I forgot you didn't know I own G. Richards' and I live in an apartment above the store. Christy, the girl who was working this morning, is the manager. She took my laptop upstairs for me."

Her explanation cleared up a thousand questions rattling around in his brain, except one. "Why would that cause me to question your sanity?"

Out of the corner of his eye, he saw her shrug. "It's as if I've known you forever. I forgot for a moment you don't know everything there is to know about me."

Okay. Now he felt like shit. She'd been intent on saying something nice and he'd ruined it. He'd find a way to make it up to her. "I assumed a place named G. Richards' would be owned by a guy named G. Richards."

"It was. He died. Now it's mine."

Her voice sounded tight. Since changing the subject hadn't helped, he chose to hold his silence and hope he survived the remainder of the evening.

* * * * *

Dinner went well. Kurt honestly believed he was making headway with McKenna until he tried to walk her to her door. She was having none of it. She gave him her cell phone number as if hoping it would be enough to make him go away. He wasn't backing down.

"I only want to see you safely inside." When she silently held his gaze, unmoving, he added. "Scout's honor."

She snorted but opened her door. "As if you were ever a boy scout."

"I was, actually," he muttered to himself as he climbed from the car. She didn't wait for him. Taking the stairs two at a time, he caught up with her halfway to the top of the metal staircase.

Glancing over her shoulder at him, she flashed a grin. "I really do have a Taser in my purse."

"Duly noted," he said, unable to mask his dry tone and causing McKenna to chuckle.

"It wasn't a threat. I was pointing out it wasn't necessary for you to try to keep me safe. I've been taking care of myself for a long time."

"Humor me, okay? I'm doing this for

my peace of mind, not yours."

When she began digging through her handbag, he wondered if she'd changed her mind about zapping him. Thankfully, she pulled out a set of keys instead. When she pushed open the door, the color yellow assaulted Kurt's senses. Ninety-five percent of the walls, as far as he could see, were plastered in sticky notes. It was almost blinding. Even though he didn't doubt there was a system to her madness, he couldn't see it. The musical sound of McKenna's laughter gave him the strength needed to tear his gaze away from the sight. Her eyes danced with humor.

"If you could see how horrified you look right now." She shook her head.

He tried rearranging his features. "I'm sorry." He snapped his teeth together, cutting off any further apology when she laughed harder.

"It's fine. Let your OCD flag fly. I'm not offended nor do I have any intention of changing. It's best you soak it all in now if you plan on becoming a regular visitor."

Choosing to take the statement as an invitation, he jumped on it. "I'm definitely coming back and I'm not horrified. It's not necessary for me to organize everyone's life, only mine."

"Hmm," she said, showing her obvious disbelief. "Oh good," she added, distracted by something across the room. "Christy didn't forget my laptop."

Following the line of her gaze, he spotted the device sitting on a glass-top table. Two envelopes, carefully set on their side, leaned against it. A single rose with a tiny pink card tied to it sat on top of the computer. Picking up the letters first, McKenna eyed them for a moment before tossing them in a nearby wastebasket.

A flash of humor ran through him. "Do you always throw away your mail unopened? That's how people get their identity stolen."

She shrugged. "I have a filing system."

He shook his head. "You'll end up on the news one of these days."

"As long as they don't use my driver's license photo," she said, sounding as if she was only half listening as she tugged the note loose from the flower. She read it aloud. "You remind me of a rose, soft and beautiful. Yet, you're strong and vibrant. Truly, you stand out above the rest." She paused, seeming to muse over the words before sighing. "Well. They're totally wrong but sweet nonetheless."

Kurt shook his head again, unable to do anything else. He wanted to argue, if only to give him a reason to stay. He'd given his word.

"I saw you safely inside, as promised. Thank you for spending the day with me."

*

He seemed so nervous McKenna half expected Kurt would start wiping sweaty palms on his jeans at any moment. It went against his character.

"I enjoyed myself."

His uncertain expression disappeared at her admission. "I did too. Maybe next time you're tied to my bed it will be under different circumstances."

There was the Kurt she'd come to expect. "Most likely not, I'm better unbound." Somehow, she managed to maintain her bland tone. Inside, she couldn't believe she'd said such a thing aloud. The wicked glint in his eyes was worth every ounce of mortification.

McKenna barely restrained herself from pressing a hand to her stomach to quell the growing desire. He made her want…everything.

His gaze swept over her body. Her nipples hardened. A shiver of yearning went through her. She deserved an award for keeping up an act of disinterest all day. The phantom pressure of his lips and his taste still lingered on her mouth.

"Damn. I'm regretting the whole scout's honor thing," he said more to himself. He returned to holding her stare. "Good night, McKenna."

The way he said her name caused her heart to race. She imagined he sounded the same on the edge of orgasm. He turned to leave.

"Good night, Kurt."

Lust burned in his eyes as he glanced over his shoulder and his lips curled into a mocking grin. He didn't say a word. There wasn't a need. The breathless note in her voice had given her away. He wouldn't stay. She almost hated herself in that moment as she watched him walk away. Making a show of it, he turned the lock on the doorknob before pulling it closed behind him. Even though she knew he wasn't coming back, her feet refused to budge. She was on fire. Electricity still filled the air even with him gone. Her body knew what a man such as Kurt could do for it. It ached for him. Her phone dinged. Tearing her gaze away from the wooden surface Kurt had set between them, McKenna searched for her phone. When she found it, she sucked a breath in at the waiting text.

I told you I'd walk you inside and nothing more. However, I have to go on record as saying it almost killed me.

Without that promise to protect you, I would've enjoyed every second of peeling off your clothes. The sound you made in the back of your throat when I said good night made my dick harden instantly. I want to hear it again while I'm buried inside you. Sleep on it.

Her mind raced. She'd made a noise? She didn't recall but also didn't doubt it. Sleep on it? As if she could rest with him crowding her brain. Her fingers hovered over the phone, debating. In the end, she decided simple was best.

Good night.

Tossing the phone aside, she headed for the shower. She'd forgotten to turn off her bedroom light again. It lit her path enough that she didn't bother switching on the one inside the bathroom. This man could get under her skin. The memory of the way the muscles flexed in

66

his back when he'd climbed off the bed earlier flashed across her mind. This time, she did press her hand against her stomach. Her gaze turned inward even as she twisted the handles to create the perfect water temperature. The scrape of his tongue stud brought her hand from her stomach to her lips. Her panties dampened even further. Peeling off her clothes, she hissed as her bra scraped along her tender nipples. As she stepped beneath the stream of water, the warm contact caused her to bite back a moan. Cupping her breasts, she squeezed, hoping to relieve some of the pressure. It was inevitable. Succumbing to desire, her hand slid lower. At the first brush of her wet folds, she tilted her head back, holding her breath. She moved slow, teasing herself. Smearing her juices over her clit, her hips moved in time with each stroke.

Clenching her ass, she rotated between pumping her finger inside her channel and circling the sensitized nub. His face was there, in the forefront of her mind as the pressure built. His name fell from her lips as the tingle exploded into pulsations. She locked her knees and clenched her back teeth against the waves rolling through her. Inexplicably, the hot press of tears spilled over her lashes. Kurt was the first man she'd wanted since Gray's death. She hated herself a little for it.

Chapter Three

Too few people appreciate the loveliness of a lily. It brings a burst of color in the spring when everything else around it still holds the dreariness of wintertime. You are the lily, a bright light in an otherwise bleak world.

"Awww," McKenna drawled after reading the note twice. She liked this one better than the rose. She touched the lily to her nose. To her, all flowers smelled the same with the exception of honeysuckle, which was why it was the only one she'd ever described in her stories. Kurt wasn't the type of man who would send her something sweet. From him, she would get a titillating surprise. He'd send a feather, she decided, along with the promise of stimulation and destruction.

"Ah, I see you got my gift."

At the sound of Kurt's voice, McKenna hid a grin. A shiver of anticipation ran through her. The memory of his taste filled her mind. "It's not from you," she stated without looking up from her notes. "You would never send such a cliché gift."

He chuckled. The sound caused her nipples to harden. The legs of the chair screeched across the tile as he sat down opposite her. She really wanted to look.

"I might."

She gave in to temptation. A black stocking cap covered his head and a pair of sunglasses rested on top of it. Thankfully, his muscular arms and chest were hidden from view by his wool coat. A naughty half-smile lingered on his lips. His green eyes twinkled, causing her to dampen her panties. There was a bruise across his cheekbone. She wanted to know but she wouldn't ask. "You don't seem concerned it might have come from someone I'm in a relationship with."

His gaze never left hers. "Concern implies it would matter. It does not, in fact, trouble me in the least."

The words hurt more than expected. Even though she never intended to act upon any desires, she enjoyed pretending he wanted her. Reality rarely lived up to fantasy. She shouldn't have looked at him. Glancing back down, she focused on the world she'd created for herself. Luke's character had begun to resemble Kurt somewhere along the way. The imitation of Kurt was the safer choice. She wanted to throw her notebook in the trash.

"Why?"

McKenna groaned as she met his stare once more. "Damn. I didn't mean to say that out loud."

"I read book two last night."

That was it. He didn't say anything more and she'd be damned if she asked his opinion.

"And?" Fuck. Was that her voice she heard? Apparently her willpower and brain weren't on the same page today.

"I got hit in the face."

His illogical statements fascinated her in spite of her best efforts. As much as she wanted to tell him to go away, she couldn't.

"Full-contact reading," she mused aloud. "Patent it. I think you're on to something."

He shook his head. The expression he wore spoke volumes about his questions on her sanity. "You're staring at me. I was explaining the bruise. I got hit in the face."

"This is staring." She dipped her

chin and fixed her eyes on him, unblinking. "Or this," she added, turning her face slightly away and watching him from the corner of her eye. When he smiled, she snorted. "Why would anyone hit you, especially in the face? Isn't such a thing illegal?"

"I imagine the fact I hit him first might have influenced his decision."

"Actually, I meant it should be illegal to harm such a work of art. Did you punch him last?"

He gave her a short nod. "I did. Would you like to go with me tonight?"

The fact their conversation made absolutely no sense didn't compute at all in McKenna's decision to continue it. At some point she'd set her elbows on the table and leaned even closer to him. It was only disturbing because she didn't remember doing it. He was like a magnet, drawing her in.

"Are we going somewhere in particular or was that an open-ended invitation?" Before she could blink, he shot forward. His mouth closed around her bottom lip.

That was it. He didn't attempt to deepen the kiss or press for more before backing away and standing. Only when her teeth clicked together did she realize her mouth had fallen open. She stared up at him, mute. With his hands shoved in the pockets of his coat, he winked.

"I'll pick you up at eight."

He walked away without giving her a chance to argue. Every single eye, including hers, followed him to the door. The moment it swung closed behind him, she sucked oxygen deep into her lungs. When the air expanded inside her chest, she recognized she'd not taken a single breath since the moment their lips touched. This man would kill her. He wouldn't even need to lift a finger against her. Apparently, her body was too stupid to keep working in his presence.

"Well, I'm totally not shaving my legs."

"Girl, you might want to wear some granny panties too, to be safe."

Tearing her eyes away from the door, McKenna focused on the mocha-skinned, chocolate-eyed twenty-something male sitting at the table across from her who'd spoken up. He flipped the page on his magazine, even though his gaze was locked on her.

"I could hide, get lost between now and then, or buy a chastity belt."

"Honey. A man like that owns a flashlight, a road map, and lock pick set."

McKenna dropped her forehead to

the table and released a whine to make any twelve-year-old girl proud. "I know! They're each labeled and perfectly stored in an easy-to-reach recyclable container." She was so fucked.

* * * * *

Kurt waited until the numbers on his watch read exactly eight p.m. before tapping his knuckles on her door. The moment McKenna answered his knock, Kurt pounced.

"You rearranged my belongings."

Stepping back and allowing him entry, she didn't miss a beat. "And how did that make you feel?" McKenna managed to ask the question in such a perfect imitation of a shrink, he chuckled in spite of himself. With her scolding out of the way, Kurt was able to enjoy the view. Beginning at her feet, he eyed her outfit. He lingered on all the strategic places. She shifted nervously beneath his gaze.

"You didn't say where we were going. I didn't know what to wear."

She'd chosen a dark blue cotton dress that ended at her knees, and a pair of knee-high, heeled boots. She looked smoking hot.

"You're going to work with me."

A line appeared between her eyes as she scrunched her face up in thought. "I have no idea what you do. How odd." She shrugged. "Let me get my coat."

He shook his head. She was the strangest person he'd ever met. How she'd managed to make it her entire life without ending up the victim of some serial killer was beyond him. For all she knew, he worked as a pimp or worse he could be taking her to his "other" job. As she attempted to reach past him, Kurt made the delicious discovery he was blocking the coat rack.

He sidestepped enough to make her think he was allowing her to pass. The moment she took her eyes off him, he made his move. Shifting his foot, he knocked her off balance while wrapping his arm around her waist. In usual McKenna style, she didn't react in the way he expected. Instead of an outraged protest, she leaned backward into his touch until her ass was flush against his hips.

Her voice came out sounding low and sexy as hell. "If you plan to cop a feel of someone, do it right."

She wrapped her fingers around his wrist at her waist and moved his hand upward until he was cupping her breast. He'd been right. It did overflow in his hand. A hum came from the back of her throat. That permanent limp he'd been living in fear of was one step closer to reality, as well. He moved to touch his lips to her shoulder. She stepped out of his hold.

"I guess we'd better go if you're going to get to work on time. Where did you say you worked, again?"

Counting backward from ten and biting back a whimper, he headed for the door. "I'm an underground fighter for the Warehouse District."

She stepped over the stoop seeming almost lost in thought. "Huh. I expected you to do something else entirely."

He had to know. "Such as?"

With her attention on the task of shoving her keys in her purse, she answered. "I don't know. You'd be an awesome master for some cougars at a fetish club."

Throwing his head back, Kurt

roared with laughter. He couldn't remember anyone ever causing him to have such a reaction. McKenna had managed it at least twice since they'd met. He swiped at his eyes.

"What would you say if I told you I also work security for a fetish club?"

McKenna's usual thoughtful expression didn't shift in the least at his question. "I'd say you're wasting your alpha-male talent. You should be spanking people instead of keeping them safe."

The statement aggravated him. Although, he couldn't pinpoint exactly why it bothered him. When they reached his Dodge Challenger, he reached past her to open the door. At the last second, he chose to keep going until she was pinned. He'd missed his chance earlier. It wasn't happening again. Peeling her coat and dress away from her shoulder, he touched his lips to her bare skin. Chill bumps rose beneath his mouth. He wondered if it was from his touch or the cold. Shifting, he placed another light kiss against the side of her neck. It hit him. He knew exactly why her statement crawled under his skin.

She shouldn't want to share him. "I'm nobody's Alpha-on-demand. When I take someone, it's because it's what I want, the way I want it. Understood?"

She shivered. Damn it. He still didn't know if it was from the cold. Giving up, he helped her into the car. He circled around and slipped behind the wheel. The moment his ass hit the seat, McKenna shocked him by apologizing.

"I'm sorry. As I was replaying my statement in my mind, I realized it sounded as if I was implying you should whore yourself out. I apologize, because you're worth so much more."

A mixture of aggravation and tenderness ran through him. She still didn't understand why she'd upset him but she did care. It was more than anyone else gave him. His jumbled emotions carried him all the way to the Warehouse District in silence. A swarm of people gathered outside the building. After helping McKenna from the car, he put his head down, doing his best to barrel a path through the crush.

Kurt almost made it to the door before realizing McKenna was gone. Whipping around, he searched the crowd with his eyes. When he caught a glimpse of her, he barely stopped his jaw from dropping. Standing on her toes, she held the lapels of some dude's jacket clenched between her hands. Her nose buried in the crook of his neck. Rage caused the gap between them to disappear before Kurt realized he'd taken a step.

"McKenna."

Even to his ears, Kurt sounded furious. She flashed a smile over her shoulder, dismissing him. The guy she held didn't spare him a glance.

"What did you say it was called again?"

The man's hooded gaze never left McKenna. A tiny grin hovered on his lips as he answered. "Gentlemen Only."

She smacked him on the arm. "I'll never remember that."

"Here," he said, reaching inside his jacket and pulling out two cards along with a pen. He handed them over. "My email address is at the bottom. If you write your name and contact information on the back of the other card, we can keep in touch. I'll make sure you get a reminder."

He added a wink. Kurt realized something vital. McKenna had never met this man before in her life.

"That's an awesome idea," McKenna agreed, doing as instructed. Kurt bit back a growl. She was seriously giving her number to some other dude while out with Kurt. With information exchanged, McKenna gave him a quick wave goodbye before rejoining Kurt.

"What the hell was that?" Was that his voice? Damned if he didn't sound like he was getting ready to rip into her. He was never, ever jealous. Fuck it. He was now.

"Oh my gosh! That guy smelled better than anyone alive. I had to know what cologne he was wearing. I'm totally using it in my next book."

"You gave your contact info to a complete stranger."

He hoped by saying it aloud, McKenna would understand how crazy her actions were. She shrugged.

"Do you have any sense of self-preservation? Don't answer that," he said before she could say anything to piss him off further. How had she lived this long? "I mean, seriously?" He added before he could stop himself. "That guy will be jacking off to this encounter for a week. Do you even know what happens to women who look like you when left at a man's mercy? Don't answer that either," he said, turning away and heading for the door. He needed to get his temper under control.

"Not every man who is nice to me wants to fuck me."

He didn't have any trouble making out her muttered words even with the mass of people surrounding them. His feet froze to the ground. The sudden change of motion caused McKenna to walk into his back.

He spun, meeting her gaze. "Uh. Yeah. They do."

"You don't," she shot back.

Wow. She was really dense. "Uh. Yeah. I do."

She was shaking her head before the final word left his lips. "I'm not saying you'd turn me down if I threw myself at you. Then again, I'm not sure you'd turn anyone down. As far as you wanting me in particular, I don't think that's true."

He moved in close enough that she was forced to tilt her head back to continue holding his stare. "I take back the apology I sent in my email. Not only are you crazy, you're also an idiot." Her lips parted on a gasp of outrage. It worked against her. Snagging her ass with one hand and her neck with the other, he hauled her body flush against his. He sealed his mouth over hers. Delving inside, he stroked her tongue and swallowed her surprised cry. He hummed against her lips as her flavor coated his taste buds. Electricity surged through him going straight to his cock. It lengthened. Ripping his mouth away, he touched his lips to the shell of her ear. Uncaring of who was watching or about the people forced to move around them to enter the building, Kurt held her in place. In a sultry tone, he told McKenna exactly what he pictured since meeting her.

"Fucking you wouldn't be enough. I want to feel your hot channel pulsing around my dick, your moans filling my ears. The sensation of your hard nipples against my bare chest is something I crave with a desperation I've never known. I've seen the way your eyes glaze over when your focus turns inward. It drives me insane because I want to be the reason for that expression." He traced the line of her ear with his tongue. "On second thought, I've decided you're right. I don't want to fuck you. I want to consume you, own you."

She clutched his t-shirt, holding onto him when he would've stepped away. Going up on her toes, McKenna touched her lips to the bare skin showing above his collar. It was the first time she'd done anything he took as being real. In an instant, he knew she did desire him but for some reason, she didn't welcome the emotion.

"You shouldn't want me." She whispered the words as if they were painful. "I'm not a good person."

She released him. In his shock, he let her go.

The women were staring at her. McKenna could feel their gazes boring into her skin. When she'd finally managed to convince Kurt she didn't have any intention of expounding on her reasons for avoiding his advances, he'd given in. Escorting her inside, he led her straight to two women who seemed to find her fascinating. After introducing the women as the wives of some men he knew, Kurt had abandoned her to prepare for his match.

Unable to stand another second of their combined intense gawking, she faced them. There wasn't a hint of remorse on their faces. Both continued looking at her unabashedly. The short brown-haired girl, Kerry, was the first to break.

"I want details."

"Fuck that," Mandy, her blonde counterpart, growled. "I want pictures."

They'd already lost her. "Are we naming random shit we want? If so, then I want minions."

Both women blinked in confusion, as if she were the one speaking in riddles. "Kurt has never introduced us to one of his dates before," Kerry said.

Mandy nodded. "I don't even think he has dates, per se."

McKenna thought over their statements before adding her agreement. "It would be exhausting making sure your socks always matched. Not to mention, I wouldn't be surprised to learn it took four hours to get anywhere with Kurt after he touched every doorknob three times."

"Oh. Now I see it."

"Yep. There it is," Mandy agreed. In unison, they both switched their attention to the cage.

Damn. She'd done it again. People

either loved her or hated her. No matter which way they leaned, they all agreed on one thing—she was off her rocker. In this instance, it kind of sucked. She wasn't sure why she wanted these women to like her but she did. There was no help for it. She might be strange but she was smart. Pulling out her cell phone, she sent Kurt a text, hoping against hope he still had his phone on him.

McKenna: *I need a nude photo of you.*

Kurt: *Will end up on the net?*

She felt moved to be honest. *Possibly.*

In a matter of seconds, three images appeared on the phone's screen. They'd obviously been taken recently but not tonight. McKenna almost swallowed her tongue. Holy Hell. She bent closer to the screen. Was that a piercing in his junk? It was, she decided after a minute of study. Almost reluctant now that they were in her possession, McKenna kept the best of the three open and handed the phone to Mandy.

She didn't disappoint. "Oh. My. Fucking. Gawd!" She tilted the phone several angles while she and Kerry huddled together to get a good view. It seemed the pair had been rendered speechless. After several minutes of ogling and drooling over Kurt's picture, Mandy handed her phone back. Both women wore matching evil grins.

"Wow girl," Kerry sighed. "That's deliciousness."

"Yeah it is," she agreed as she snuck another peek at the pic.

Kerry and Mandy moved in, forming a wall and blocking out the people around them. Kerry pulled her phone out.

"This is my husband."

McKenna wasted no time getting in on that action. Sultry blue eyes and an angelic face did nothing to hide the man's devilry. She fanned her face.

"Whoa."

Kerry's smile turned luminous at the compliment. "Come on, Mandy," Kerry goaded. "You're on the hook here too."

With a childlike giggle, she pulled a digital camera out of her bag. "I'm a professional photographer," she explained at McKenna's questioning look.

She huddled even closer to the women. This would be good. Good turned out to be an understatement. McKenna gawked at the images and ended up giggling like a schoolgirl. It was all an act. They had gorgeous men. There wasn't a need for her to feign a reaction but her mind stayed with Kurt. The hard lines of his body against hers lingered at the forefront of all her thoughts. He didn't know how badly she wanted to cave. Since the moment they met, he consumed her fantasies. Her stomach cramped. She couldn't watch her passion kill someone else. The first bell rang. Mandy jumped and readied her camera.

"Yay! My husband's up."

Turning her attention to the cage, McKenna was amazed by the difference in the man who was gearing up to fight from the one who Mandy captured in her shots. This man was hardened and unforgiving. She couldn't imagine the willowy blonde standing at her shoulder surviving life with such a man but her happiness was apparent. Giving up on puzzling out their relationship, she concentrated on the action instead.

It was fascinating, disturbing yet

engrossing. The sound of fists against flesh was louder than she expected. Greed hung in the air heavily enough that McKenna swore she could smell it. Everywhere she looked, she saw dead-eyed patrons who smiled with malicious glee at each pound of flesh doled out for their entertainment.

Mandy's husband, Knox, finished off his opponent in what McKenna would've sworn was record time. Mandy assured her it wasn't. The moment Knox's fight ended, Kerry's husband, Dane, appeared at her side with two other men in tow. They were equal in height but while one was similar to Kurt in size and bulk, the other man had the lean muscle of a runner. In McKenna's opinion, they were both the epitome of masculine perfection. Kerry introduced the Kurt-sized male as her brother-in-law, Rhys. The beautiful one was Asher. Although she felt certain she was staring, she couldn't seem to stop. To make matters worse, Asher smelled even better than the man from the parking lot. She tried to behave. Honestly, she did.

"Can I sniff your skin?"

Every person within hearing distance turned to stare. Her face heated. For the first time in memory, she found herself explaining her odd behavior.

"I'm an author. It's an issue."

Rhys smiled kindly. "No need to explain. I completely understand your pain. He's a bit irresistible." McKenna wanted to smack herself for not seeing it sooner. They were together and not in a platonic way. Shit. She'd really hadn't meant to hit on the dude's man. He was still beaming as he waved her closer.

"Come here. Seriously," Rhys added when she didn't move. Asher shook his head but he was smiling as he made room for her to stand between them. The closer she got the harder it became for her to hold back.

"Wow," she said, leaning in to get a better whiff. "How the hell do you resist him?"

Asher's eyes twinkled with suppressed humor while the two of them exclaimed over his cologne. "You are both quite outrageous. Whatever shall I do with the two of you for the entire night?"

At his question, McKenna turned back to Rhys. "Holy fucking shit! He has a sexy accent too?"

"I know, right?" Rhys winked as he added, "I'm a lucky guy."

She smelled Asher's jacket again. Her mind went fuzzy as a memory pricked at her brain. "I know what it is. You're a chocolate-covered cinnamon apple."

Asher released a low chuckle. "How did someone as refreshing as you end up with this rough bunch tonight?"

"She's dating Kurt," Kerry answered before McKenna had a chance. Asher stiffened. His gaze shifted from perusing the room to her face. There was something in his expression she couldn't decipher and his lips parted as if he meant to say something. She cut him off. "I'm not dating Kurt. I guess I'm technically on a date with him now but we're not dating. Unless you consider the one time I went to his apartment so he could tie me to the bed a date but we didn't have sex. Although we did sleep together and he did feed me afterward. Fuck it. I'm dating Kurt. How the hell did that happen?"

Everyone was staring at her again. Fortunately, Kerry nodded as if she understood. "I ended up married once under similar circumstances. He asked if I wanted to get something for dinner and I said, 'I could eat'. Next thing I knew I was repeating my wedding vows in the line of a drive-thru wedding chapel. The hamburger was good."

"How odd," McKenna mused aloud. "I also got married in a Vegas drive-thru. Of course, my marriage didn't end well. He died so I don't think it's any reflection on drive-thru weddings in general. They can hardly be blamed for it."

Kerry looked thoughtful. "Huh. The man I married died too."

"Perhaps someone should do a study on the mortality rate of men who marry Vegas-style."

When Kerry seemed to consider McKenna's suggestion, she felt, for once, as if someone understood her odd thought patterns. After a couple of minutes, Kerry nodded. "He did die in a motorcycle accident. It could be the whole always-on-the-move factor."

"My husband killed himself."

"Oh." Kerry appeared taken aback. "A coincidence then, I suppose."

A loud voice rang through the speaker system—thankfully—ending the conversation before it became more awkward.

"All right ladies and gentlemen, I hope you've gotten your wagers in. All further bets are now closed. This next match we have our own Kurt Travis against World Divisional, No Rival fighter Brian Johnson. The legal boys do enjoy playing in our yard from time to time. This should be a good one, folks."

As the announcements continued, Kurt appeared through the doorway of the cage. The mass of people surrounding

McKenna shoved forward. When the cheers died down a notch, she could hear the man still carrying on over the microphone, adding fuel to the crowd's excitement.

"In case we have anyone visiting tonight from World Divisional, hoping to see some real action, let me go over the rules. Here at Warehouse District, there's only one. When you step into the cage, it's to the death."

Kurt's face could've been cut from marble for all the emotion he showed over the pronouncement. She felt sick.

"They don't literally mean 'to the death', do they?" she asked no one in particular. Rhys patted her on the arm. "It's a mentality rule. These are no-holds-barred matches. Fighters are expected to face-off with a kill-or-be-killed, anything-to-win attitude. You fight until someone goes down and doesn't get up."

"Oh." His explanation did sound better than what she pictured in her head but not much. Since Rhys' build was similar to Kurt's and he knew the rules, she was curious. "Do you fight here too?"

"No. I'm World Divisional, the same as Kurt's opponent. We have rules. Not many, mind you but enough to keep us alive to compete another day."

McKenna thought of a thousand more questions but the bell rang, drawing her attention back to the action. The man facing off against Kurt had lovely chocolate-colored skin and a look of determination. His muscular jaw flexed as he bounced on his toes. All the men were well-kept machines. She wanted to sigh but she was too nervous. As dark as McKenna's writing was, she didn't much care for actual violence.

In a move almost too quick for the eye, Brian struck hard and fast by landing a blow to the side of Kurt's head. Rhys sucked in a sharp breath.

"I told him not to do that."

If McKenna was being honest, the move made her a little angry. His one punch made her realize she didn't like anyone hitting Kurt. In an attempt at calming her temper, she chose to concentrate on Rhys instead.

"Why?"

Before Rhys could answer her question, Kurt threw two sharp jabs. Both made contact, snapping Brian's head back and drawing blood.

"Never mind," McKenna grumbled. She understood. Brian had pissed Kurt off. He would be twice as vicious. On a leap, Kurt's knee sank into the other man's abdomen. "Oh dear. Kurt's not likely to let him off easy now."

"Exactly." The bleak note to Rhys' voice said a lot.

Taking advantage of Brian's scramble to recover, Kurt spun. His back kick caught Brian in the jaw. He went down. To McKenna's surprise, he sprang back to his feet before Kurt could attempt a pin.

Kurt wore an expression McKenna couldn't think of any way to describe. Since it was her job to paint mental pictures with words, her loss seemed even more significant. The look in his eyes went beyond anger. Something dark had been unleashed from inside him. From the way Rhys stiffened at her side, she knew he'd seen it as well.

"He should have stayed down." McKenna silently agreed.

Proving them both right, almost as

if choreographed, Kurt snagged Brian's wrist mid-swing. In one fluid motion, he tugged the man forward until he face-planted on the mat. Twisting, while still holding Brian's arm, Kurt brought his heel down on Brian's shoulder blade. It seemed the entire room chose the same moment to draw a breath. Everything fell silent. The cracking of bone was audible as Brian's arm snapped.

McKenna knew, as long as she lived, she would never forget the sound Brian made in his pain. Rhys strung together a list of curse words she'd never heard used in the same sentence as he raced toward the cage's door. The place exploded into motion. Rhys and Asher were on the mat, attending to Brian in a matter of seconds. The crowd pressed against her as each individual fought to get a better view. McKenna couldn't move. Her feet cemented to the floor. Time seemed to slow. Her vision darkened around the edges until she was staring at Kurt through a tunnel. He refused to let the official lift his arm in victory. Instead, he turned her way, searching the crowd with his eyes until he found her. For a single, unguarded moment, McKenna saw something inside him. It caused the oxygen to leave her lungs. He was scared of himself and he needed her. She was moving in his direction before making any conscious decision to do so. He met her at the edge of the mat.

The power of his passion, the adrenaline pumping through his veins, both of those things were almost tangible. He flinched when she reached for his hand. It didn't keep him from squeezing her fingers when she tugged him forward. A muscle jumped in his jaw. He eyed her as if expecting she'd run screaming from the building at any moment even as he allowed her to tow him from inside the cage. She walked backward, holding his gaze. She wasn't afraid.

"Where's your stuff, baby?"

The endearment seemed to snap him from his haze. He blinked. "The locker room."

"Let's get it. Okay?"

"Ich würde Dich nie verletzen."

"Baby, I don't speak anything but English. You'll have to give me a small break here."

"I would never hurt you."

A sharp pain hit her in the chest. "I wish I could make you the same promise." Somehow, McKenna managed to get Kurt to the locker room. Unwilling to take any chances, she sucked in a deep breath for courage and simply strolled inside with him as if she belonged. She did her best not to look right or left. Men being men, they postured but didn't bat an eye over her presence. They certainly didn't suggest she leave. Kurt had gone quiet but he dutifully tugged a shirt over his head and pulled on a pair of slick workout pants.

"Give me your keys."

"I'm not an invalid, McKenna. I can still take care of you."

Holding out her hand, palm up, she wiggled her fingers at him. With a growl, he gave in to her silent demand. Several people tried stopping them on the way out the door. McKenna kept a tight hold on Kurt as she barreled past them. It wasn't until they were halfway to her apartment that she realized he'd fully withdrawn from her. He became like a stranger. The change was almost palpable. In light of the situation, McKenna made an important discovery. It was cold on the outside when Kurt decided to shut someone out. She hated it. The time had come for extreme measures.

He dutifully followed her inside her apartment, watching with an expression akin to horror as she stuffed his car keys inside her purse. She suppressed a grin. If she'd thrown them in the sewer, she didn't doubt he'd have gone after them. As most men were, he'd been rendered helpless by a simple zippered leather handbag.

*

"How am I supposed to get home?"

McKenna hung her coat and purse on the rack. "You're not going home." Silence filled the air between them as he tried to decipher her meaning. Before he could ask, she added. "You owe me an apology."

He dropped his gaze to the toes of his shoes. Shit. He'd ruined everything. "I'm sorry. I shouldn't have put you in this position."

She kicked out of her boots. "I'm not talking about that." Snagging the hem of her dress, McKenna peeled it over her head. His mind went blank but his heartbeat quickened. "Every time we're together, you get me wet. The problem is, you never do anything to remedy it." She unhooked her black lace bra and tossed it on top of her dress on the floor. "Say you're sorry."

Her body was so much better than he'd ever imagined. And he had an awesome imagination. McKenna was a goddess.

"I'm sorry."

Hooking her thumbs in the band of her thong, she slipped it down her hips.

"You don't sound apologetic."

Kurt had an epiphany. McKenna's constant conversational tone was a mask. The beautifully sexual mind he'd seen at work in her books stayed locked behind the quirky face she showed the world. They weren't two separate parts of her. For some reason, she chose to hide. She fascinated him, captivated him.

"From the bottom of my heart, I sincerely beg your forgiveness."

"I'd have an easier time believing you if I wasn't the only one not wearing any clothes."

His jacket slid from his shoulders. Her eyes hooded. The shirt disappeared from his back. His attention locked on her. Everything else was secondary. For once, his brain didn't control his every action. McKenna owned him now. As he toed off his shoes, she turned away, trailing down the hall. No doubt, she expected him to follow. She was right. He still owed her an apology. As if attached to an invisible leash, Kurt stayed on her heels. The moment a steel-framed bed came into view, he sprang, pinning McKenna facedown beneath him.

"Tell me what I did wrong so I can fix it. Which parts of you ache when I leave?"

His voice sounded ravaged, even to him. It was nothing compared to McKenna's when she answered.

"My breasts feel heavy."

The length of his hardened cock tried pushing its way past his waistband. He opened his mouth over her spine between her shoulder blades.

McKenna gasped. "Oh God."

At the exclamation, he burrowed his hands underneath her, kneading the breasts she claimed he'd neglected. Her beaded nipples scraped along his palms.

"My panties dampen," she added.

In his mind, he could already taste her cream coating his tongue. He growled against her skin as he counted her vertebrae with his tongue until he reached the base of her spine. Clasping her hips, he urged her upward and onto her knees. He sank his teeth into the soft flesh of her ass, drawing a gasp from her lungs. Brushing his lips over the spot in apology, he hesitated, giving her a chance to deny him. When she didn't, he slammed the window of opportunity closed. Reaching around, he pinched her clit between his thumb and forefinger. He circled her asshole with his tongue, once, before tracing the line to her pussy. A moan tore from her lips. She moved against him. He dipped his tongue inside. Feminine salt filled his mouth and his stomach growled. Kurt was starving. McKenna was the most decadent of meals for a man too long denied. Lapping at her juices, Kurt circled her nub.

"My channel feels empty without your dick," McKenna said on a ragged breath.

She left him wrecked. His chest hit her back. The sound of the air leaving her lungs as he squashed her beneath his weight sounded loud in the otherwise silent room. He didn't recall moving. The confession had caused his body to move before his mind accepted it was happening. Her ass cradled his erection through the workout pants. The thin barrier between them was the only thing stopping him from taking what he wanted. He was holding on to control by a thread. His passion and her confession brought a hint of reality. Tonight, he didn't want to pleasure her and leave. He needed to be inside her. They had a problem. This had not been a part of his plan.

"I didn't bring any condoms with me." He almost felt sick at the admission. There hadn't been anyone he truly wanted in years, until McKenna. Now she was within reach and he couldn't have her.

"I'm on the pill."

His lungs ceased working. Were they really discussing this? Easing up, he urged her onto her back. He needed to look into her eyes. Brushing her hair away from her face, he held her cheek in his hand and her gaze with his.

"I have to get tested every six months for most diseases to continue competing at Warehouse District since we come into contact with one another's blood. I'm clean." He paused wondering if he was brave enough to tell her everything. In the end, he wanted her to know it all. Most of all, he needed her to realize she was unique to him. "Not that those tests matter in the least since I haven't had sex with anyone in over three years." Her eyebrows nearly hit her hairline but she didn't call him a liar. It did make him feel as if he should add. "I'm not saying I haven't done other things with the exception of actual intercourse."

"Why?"

Leave it to McKenna to need to know. She deserved to. "You saw me tonight. I'm intense and I can't control it. If I don't keep myself locked down, my emotions take over my whole life. Most people can't handle me when I'm firing on all cylinders. You can." He waited for her argument but it didn't come. Since he was all in now, he kept going with the endless confessions. "Since I saw you sitting there barefoot, in the wintertime and in a coffee shop, I haven't been able to stay away. All the things about me I can't control have fired to life since the first moment I met you. I want to be inside you so badly right now the thought of missing out makes me physically ill but I also know myself too well. It won't be enough for me. I'm passionate. I'm obsessive. I won't stop until you agree to keep me. If this is a one-night stand for you then I'd prefer to skip it."

He half expected her to kick him out of her bed. She shocked him by chuckling. "You do all of those things now. How are you expecting life to change after tonight?"

He traced a circle around her nipple, watching as she struggled to keep her breathing under control. "I'm being serious, McKenna. Tonight, I wanted to tell Kerry and Mandy you're mine. The next time we leave this place, I want to be able to say it and know it's true. This need for you to know you're always welcome wherever I am is driving me insane. I also want to know I'm welcome wherever you are."

His dick was having a separate conversation with his brain about how stupid he was. There was a pain in his chest warning him of how much it would hurt if she turned him away.

"You can't leave me here alone. I'm waiting for you to show me what the purpose is for those piercings I saw in your pictures."

He knew it was her way of giving in while holding onto her pride. His heart soared. He didn't need to steal her pride away to find his footing. He pushed his pants down his hips before lowering his head. He needed to taste her lips. Pausing an inch from her delicious mouth, he demanded she give him the words he needed.

"Tell me you belong to me."

She buried her fingers in his hair, holding him in place. "You're so beautiful."

He scoffed at the words. "It should've been me telling you how gorgeous you are."

"I beat you to it. Now would you please show me the value of those kinky piercings? It's freezing in here. I need you to keep me warm."

The first mention of any discomfort on her part had him moving. He covered her with his body. There was no way he would allow his woman to get a chill. He'd have her promise another day.

Drawing her hand downward between them, he wrapped her fingers around his shaft, guiding her to the first stud. It was in the tip of his cock. He hissed through his teeth as she toyed with it. "This one is for my pleasure." Urging her hand farther down, he steered her toward the heavy silver ring at the base of his cock. "This one is for your pleasure. As for my other piercings, you'll have to find and figure out those for yourself."

Sharp breaths shuddered from her lips. "A challenge then? Can I take you up on it later?" She fisted his erection, stroking him. "Right now, I want this buried inside me. I'm done playing."

She thought they were playing? How cute. Not by a long shot. Surging forward, he opened his mouth over hers.

*

Inside, McKenna was shaking. She hadn't slept with anyone since Gray died. Taking her clothes off in front of Kurt had been scary as hell. Now she was getting ready to welcome him inside her body. A thousand emotions crowded her brain. She could say no. Kurt shifted, taking her with him. In a flash of movement, she was the one on top, straddling his hips. The control belonged to her. She could back down. Bracing her weight on her palms, her hair fell forward, creating a curtain around them, giving the illusion they were inside a private cocoon. It was intimate. Up close, Kurt's eyes were such a light green they almost seemed amber.

The tips of his fingers trailed down her spine. She couldn't back down. There had never been any real chance of doing so. His hands encircled her hips, urging her upward. Dropping her gaze to his kiss-swollen lips, McKenna beat back her fear.

"You're so wet it's killing me."

The ripple of his abs against her

sensitized nub caused her channel to pulse with need. It also reminded her of how solid he was at the apex of her thighs. He was a real person, with feelings and expectations. Her chest tightened. She always destroyed real people. Slipping her hand between them, she positioned the head of his cock against her opening. Meeting his stare, she licked her lips nervously but gave him what she knew he wanted.

"I do belong to you."

His pupils dilated at her confession. The wide crown of his cock pressed inside her as his hips left the mattress. Pushing against him, she accepted all of him. He filled her completely, stretching her wide. His nostrils flared. Every line of his face hardened, becoming hawklike. The transformation ignited a different spark of fear in McKenna's chest. He looked deadly.

She rocked against him. The piercing he promised was for her pleasure, was. It slid along her slit, hitting her clit at the perfect angle. The delicious friction stole away all of her doubts. Kurt's eyes fell closed. His lips parted on a breath. McKenna needed to taste them.

Capturing his bottom lip between her teeth, she allowed his dick to slip almost completely away before sitting back against it. She went slow, doing her best to torture Kurt. His hands rested on her hips but he didn't attempt to control her movements. The tingle growing between her legs held her focus. She could hear the mewling sounds coming from her mouth. It was out of her control. Kurt's tongue brushing hers, his cock pumping inside her and the smell of his skin all added strength to the pressure building. Balancing on the edge of ecstasy, she tightened her inner muscles around his dick. He growled. The sound triggered something that sent her flying apart. Light exploded behind her eyes. All the air left her lungs, leaving her gasping.

"Thank fuck." Kurt's curse was the only warning she got before her back hit the mattress. With her leg over his shoulder, he surged forward, hitting something at the perfect angle. Another orgasm slammed into her, taking her by surprise. She tore at the sheets beneath her hands in an attempt to cling to some sanity. Kurt was all-consuming. She tasted him on her tongue. Her lips stung from his kisses and her body tingled as if crawling with tiny flames. The sound of his moans filled her ears. Her nostrils prickled with his scent. She was captivated by the sight of him possessing her. Even in a haze of ecstasy, the way his every muscle rippled in time with his movements left her fascinated. His locked jaw jumped in time with his cock as he came. McKenna's heart slammed against the wall of her chest at the vision he presented. His gaze never left hers. He homed in on her with a laser-like precision. The oxygen in her lungs froze. He'd not lied to her about his intensity. Inexplicably, McKenna wanted to cry. She could love him.

Love always destroyed her.

Chapter Four

A slash of sunlight fell across his face, startling Kurt awake. He blinked at the sight in amazement. The tightness in his muscles brought the prior night's events rushing back. Flashes of McKenna's delicious body floated through his mind. The memory of her moans and tight heat tugging at his cock caused his already hard dick to twitch. She was gone but her scent lingered on the sheets. Twice now, he'd slept soundlessly at her side. There was something about McKenna. She stole away his demons. He'd been in a dark place when his temper snapped in the cage. Even in the face of his insanity, she'd not backed down. McKenna charged into the place inside him where his mind retreated, refusing to leave. She could easily destroy him if she decided she didn't want him any longer. Pushing aside the panic that threatened to overcome him at the realization, he scrubbed his hands over his face. Where had she gone? Following the smell of coffee, Kurt went in search of McKenna without bothering to cover his nudity. Clothes were pointless. For his purposes, he wouldn't need them.

When he spied her standing in the kitchen, he soaked in the view. With wet hair dripping down her back and a towel tucked under her arms, she bent close to something set on the counter. He couldn't make out what she was doing since her body blocked it from view. It didn't matter. She made his skin feel too tight. Moving closer to her task, McKenna's towel slipped an inch lower down her back. His heart sped up. Without realizing it, Kurt's feet carried him across the room. She drew him in without his permission. For the first time, he understood how a moth felt when it spotted a flame. He was helpless to resist.

A moan escaped her as he ripped the towel away, replacing it with his body. The sound caused his eyes to fall closed. She wasn't surprised. It was impossible to predict her reaction to anything since she never behaved as expected. She drove him insane, left him unbalanced. He couldn't get enough. All his practiced seduction went out the window, replaced with need.

"I'm sorry. I want you too bad to go slow." He pushed her shoulders away as he hauled her hips toward him, forcing McKenna to bend at the waist. Sliding his crown along her slit, he released an inner sigh of relief when he found her wet. He didn't have the strength to wait. Years of hard-earned self-control flew out the window.

Her inner walls gave way as he slid inside. Staring down between their bodies, he watched as he slipped almost completely away, juices coating his dick. McKenna held on to the edge of the counter. She pushed against him. He gripped her hips, keeping her in place and forcing her to accept his will.

McKenna growled and he chuckled at the sound. "You're a tease," McKenna snapped.

She had no idea. Kurt buried his fingers in McKenna's hair. Tugging her head back, he sank his teeth into the soft flesh of her neck. She whimpered. If possible, he hardened even more at the sound. She was killing him.

"How far are you willing to go?"

Inner muscles tightened around his member at the question. "Anywhere you want to take me."

"I haven't found a thing I'm unwilling to try. Be careful what you agree to do." Her back arched, pushing him deeper. She was panting. "I want it all."

It was all the permission needed. She'd sealed her fate. Pulling free, he snagged her around the waist, easily tossing her over his shoulder. Heading for the bedroom, she didn't make any protest. Her hands cupped his ass as he walked, making him smile. McKenna was exactly as naughty as he liked. In one motion, Kurt laid her on the edge of the bed, knees spread wide. With his gaze locked on her face, he probed her ass. His dick was coated with her juices. Using her moisture against her, he pushed past the tight ring of muscles. Circling her clit with his thumb, he kept her aroused in hopes of offsetting any pain involved. There was an expression on her face he couldn't put a name to but it did something to his stomach. It fluttered. He wanted to tighten his abs, staving off the sensation. Her pupils dilated. She visibly fought for every breath through parted lips. Before her, there had never been a single person he wanted to keep. McKenna belonged to him.

When he was fully seated inside, he held still. He knew he didn't need to move. The squeeze of her ass would pull him into release once he gave her the pleasure she deserved.

"Are you okay?"

The rough note in his voice almost sounded inhuman. She gripped his forearms, digging her nails in. Her hips left the mattress.

"Fuck me."

Between her expression, the feel of her body surrounding his and the sight of her beautiful bare breasts, something inside his mind snapped at the demand. His intent to hold still flew out the window. His dick pounding inside her, his fingers pumping her channel before circling her nub, and the sounds of her cries, all of those details barely penetrated his lust. She made him half insane to have her in every way. As his balls drew up tight, he knew there was no way in hell she was leaving this bed again today.

She didn't. By the time darkness fell throughout McKenna's room, she'd found all his piercings.

* * * * *

The gym at the Vegas Veterans rehabilitation center didn't smell the same as any place most fighters trained. Antiseptic and cleaning solution hung in the air. Kurt barely registered the scent any longer. The place was also brighter than most training facilities. No Rival and Grid Iron were both dark testosterone-filled places. The Veterans center was full of determination. It packed every square inch of the sterile facility. Terry Richards was already waiting for him. At one time, Terry had been the US middleweight champion before losing the title to Rhys Collier. The soldiers loved him. He was hard. It was something to which each of them could relate. Sweat coated Terry's skin as he sparred with Cameron. One-half of Cameron North's body was covered with extensive scarring. That and the two fingers missing from his right-hand were what was left behind after he attempted to save a small child who'd been set on fire by rebels in Afghanistan. None of those events managed to slow the man down. His will to live gave Kurt hope.

"You're smiling," Terry bit out

between ducking blows. Kurt hadn't realized it. After a moment of trying to rearrange his features, he gave up.

"So I am."

Both men seemed immobilized by his admission. As if by silent mutual agreement, the match ended. Their focus locked on him. Cameron eyed him suspiciously. The slight golden tint to his hair captured the light as he tilted his head to one side, as if trying to decide what was different. Terry smiled. Even then, his usual cynical look didn't leave his eyes.

"So who is it?"

Cameron's expression cleared at Terry's question. He shook his head. "Oh man. I never thought I'd live to see the day someone snagged you."

In spite of his best efforts, a smile tugged harder at the corners of Kurt's mouth. He didn't alleviate their curiosity.

"Come on. I'd tell you."

Kurt glanced up at the ceiling for a second, seeking guidance. "If you plan to keep digging until I tell you something, her name is McKenna."

Cameron released a low whistle. "That's a sexy name. Is she a stripper?"

Kurt ground his back teeth, biting back a growl. Even the hint of another man thinking of her in such a way pissed him off.

At the sound, Cameron rocked back on his heels. "Whoa. You're really serious about this one." Kurt's good humor returned. Cameron's original opinion was based on Kurt's past behavior. He could hardly blame the man. His temper would always be his biggest downfall.

"She writes erotica," he admitted. Tossing Cameron a wink, he let him know there weren't any hard feelings. Terry's spine visibly stiffened. He shoulders squared. There was something in his expression, or rather there wasn't. His face had gone completely blank. The man had always been a bit of a mystery to Kurt. They weren't friends but then, he didn't think Terry had friends. Most likely, being the champion had taught him some tough lessons. Everyone was after something when you were on top. Terry wasn't a Vet. He'd simply showed up one day and hadn't stopped volunteering since. If anyone knew anything about him, they weren't talking.

Terry waved him away. "Get changed. Nobody likes a lovesick fool." Tapping Cameron's shoulder, Terry motioned for their match to resume. As happy as Kurt was, he almost felt guilty. All the years of black moods and wretched nightmares had been Kurt's punishment for the lives he'd cut short. Part of him wanted to revel in finding a light in his darkness. Another part of him wondered if he deserved any comfort at all. In the locker room, Kurt tugged his shirt over his head and froze. Staring at a poster declaring Uncle Sam needed him, Kurt turned Terry's words over in his mind. He called Kurt lovesick. Was he? McKenna would be the death of him.

* * * * *

February

There was a kid on fire. He couldn't have been more than seven years old. How could anyone do such a thing to a child? Cameron tackled him, attempting to beat out the flames. Whatever accelerant had been used, it wasn't letting up. The heat from the blaze burned so brightly, it scorched Kurt's skin from five feet away.

137

The pain on Cameron's part had to be massive but the man didn't make a sound. It was almost a relief when the high-pitched screams came to an end. His eyes stung. He couldn't tell any longer if it was due to the smoke or holding back tears. The scent of burning flesh assailed his senses. The screams began again. Why wouldn't they stop? Dear God. Let him die already. Lifting his rifle, he fired two shots, ending the boy's suffering. Still the screeching wouldn't cease. Something soft hit his face. It didn't hurt but it was enough to cause his eyes to fly open. McKenna hovered over him. She appeared half crazed. Sweat glistened on her face, causing strands of blonde hair to cling to her skin. His heart raced. There was no air. She was more important than oxygen.

"What's wrong, baby?" His voice came out sounding as if he'd chewed on broken glass.

"You were screaming. I couldn't get you to wake up. Holy shit." She brushed a shaky hand across her eyes.

Damn. He'd been dreaming again. Pressing the heels of his hands against his eyeballs, Kurt did his best to wipe away the picture in his head. He saw stars but the images were still there. He'd almost be willing to burn out his retinas if it would take the memories away.

"I had a bad dream," he told McKenna. He knew she was waiting for answers. There were things he couldn't tell her. She buried her face against his chest.

"Oh my God. You scared the shit out of me."

Burying his fingers in her hair, he massaged her scalp, hoping to ease her worry. She deserved so much more than the fucked-up mess she'd gotten in him.

Her lips touched his overheated skin, lingering. The breath caught in his throat. He waited to see what she'd do next. Her tongue shot out, brushing over the same spot. The sensation caused his mind to go blank, setting him free. His focus locked on McKenna. Her hand came to rest between his legs. His dick went hard. Palming his erection, she tugged upward. Her soft skin brushed along his most sensitive nerve endings. Drawing a slow breath in through his nose, Kurt was almost scared to move. He didn't want to miss whatever she planned next.

Dipping lower, she stroked each rib with her tongue until he wondered if she was keeping count. He released her hair, allowing her the freedom to do as she pleased. Her hand trailed lower. As she rolled his balls between her fingers, his cock leaked on his stomach. Her hot mouth opened over his abs. Air hissed between his teeth at the feel of her tongue swiping over his obliques. Her hair tickled his erection with every pass. The tip of her finger toyed with his Guiche piercing. Bringing his knee up, he gave McKenna room to move. At the motion, she openly fondled the ring. It tugged at the skin near his asshole, bringing twinges of decadence. His hips left the bed.

As if it was the cue McKenna had been waiting on, she closed her lips around his dick. Gripping the sheets beneath him, Kurt tried his best to keep from forcing her to take all of him down her throat. She could and she would. Patience wasn't his strong point when it came to her. The pleasure she brought him bordered on torture. There had never been anyone who chased away the darkness before her. She made him want things again.

Right now, she made him want to fuck her mouth. No matter how hard he tried, he couldn't stop from grinding against her, urging his cock deeper. A noise came from the back of her throat. At the sound, his eyes flew open and he stared down the line of his body. The erotic vision waiting for him caused his balls to draw up tight. One of her hands moved between her legs, keeping time with the hollowing of her cheeks. Her muscles convulsed and she swallowed him with a hum. Without warning, an orgasm exploded from him. The breath left his lungs. He struggled to gulp down enough air to survive. As his brain disconnected from reality, Kurt experienced a blinding moment of clarity. He was completely in love with this woman.

* * * * *

McKenna tried to concentrate on the words on the screen. Her brain refused to cooperate. Three months. She'd let it go on for twelve whole weeks. Kurt's nightmares seemed to be getting worse. He disappeared for several hours each day. There were hundreds of secretive things about him. Intentionally, she'd avoided asking him about anything. There was a huge part of McKenna that knew if she looked too closely at Kurt's life, she wouldn't like what she learned. She'd ignored some other things as well. It was coming back to haunt her now. The news had come in at exactly two-seventeen that afternoon. She couldn't avoid the truth any longer. There also wasn't a single doubt in her mind she wouldn't be able to hang on to Kurt. He was too much of everything. Most of all, he was too good to be true.

"Come to work with me."

Kurt's cajoling words cut through McKenna's thoughts. "I have a confession. I'm not a fan of violence."

He snagged her chair, pulling it away from the desk. A wicked smile crossed his features. "Not that job."

Oh. That job. "You know I don't know how to behave. There's no way you'll be able to take me to a fetish club."

Going down on his knees, Kurt tugged her forward, circling her waist with his arms. His body pressed against the apex of her thighs. "You don't have to go inside. I don't." He nuzzled the side of her neck. The tingle between her legs became an ache. "There's this awesome alcove outside the door. No one would be able to see us."

She felt moved to point out the obvious. "Nobody can see us now." There was no way he was missing the breathless note in her tone or her hardened nipples. She wanted him. His teeth sank into her soft flesh. A moan fell from her lips. All it took was his presence and she was ready to rip the clothes off his back.

"I don't have time to do all the things I want. If you come with me, I'll have all night."

It was tempting. Reluctantly, she pushed at his shoulders until he moved away. "I'm being serious. You're working security for this place. I'm the one you'll be forced to remove from the property. Can you imagine me questioning everyone as they go in? I won't be able to help it. Plus, I really need to get some writing done. There's a deadline beating at my door."

With a groan, Kurt gave in. "Yeah. I get you."

A look passed over his face as he

came to his feet. Her rejection had wounded him. The line of the erection in his jeans distracted her. It was for her. She really wanted to give in. Her chest hurt. She needed to work. The next book in her series wouldn't get written in a darkened alcove.

"I'm sorry."

He had no idea how much she regretted missing out. She wanted to cry over the thought of how much her body needed his.

He gripped the arms of her chair, leaning in. "Don't worry over it. I'll be here the moment I get off. Until then, I want you picturing all the naughty stuff I'll do to you." He touched his lips to hers. "And I'll come up with a list of demands," he added as he opened his mouth over hers. The cinnamon flavor that was uniquely Kurt coated her tongue. There were thousands of things she wanted to say and do. Instead, she did her best to make him understand with a single kiss. Her every emotion was so strong she couldn't believe he could stand under the weight of them once she threw them his way.

His lips clung to her skin. "Think of me."

As if she had a choice.

* * * * *

He should quit this place. It was a thought that grew a little more with each day. The thrill of the hunt disappeared the moment he'd met McKenna. She made him realize what he'd been missing. It was her. The more he thought things over, the more certain he became. He was turning in his two-week notice.

"Why are you hiding back here by yourself?"

Kurt's heart slammed against the

wall of his chest. He never allowed anyone to sneak up on him. There wasn't any denying Patrick had managed it.

"Slow night," Kurt answered, pasting on his smoothest of smiles. He might have been caught unawares but he didn't have to show it.

"Good. Then you have time for me."

Fuck. "Of course." Straightening away from the wall, Kurt pulled the security pass from his back pocket. "I apologize for causing you to seek me out. It's not like me to ignore my duties," he said, intent on brushing past him and attempting to scan his pass. Before he could reach the keypad, Patrick pressed his palm against the brick, blocking his path. Kurt released an inner sigh.

"You misunderstand."

No. He really didn't. Most people were smart enough to realize Kurt didn't come back for seconds. Unfortunately, the five-foot-ten male whose clear-blue eyes had tempted him once had clearly not gotten the memo.

"I'm not known for my depth."

Patrick smirked. "I beg to differ. You're known far and wide for how deep you're willing to go." He let the words hang between them for a second before adding, "As a matter of fact, the last time we were out here, you told me in great detail exactly how far you'd take me into your throat."

If Kurt was honest with himself, he'd known this night would come. This side of Patrick was what had attracted Kurt in the first place. He'd known it was there, simmering under the surface waiting for release. Well, here it was.

"And have you been envisioning it?" Kurt wanted to kick his own ass the

149

moment the question fell from his lips. Even he didn't know where he was going with this. It was a move to stall until he thought of something better.

"Every night."

It was Kurt's turn to smirk. "Was I good?"

"Very. It's time you proved it."

Before Kurt had a chance to respond, Patrick closed the gap between them, touching his lips to Kurt's. It didn't seem to matter that he was unresponsive. Patrick simply traveled from his lips to his throat. In his shock, Kurt threw his hands up in surrender. He didn't know who he was attempting to show that he wasn't touching the man in any way since they were alone. It didn't matter. He didn't want there to be any misunderstanding.

"Whoa. Sorry to interrupt."

At the dryly spoken words, Patrick

sprang away from Kurt, flushing. His embarrassment over getting busted kissing another man had nothing on Kurt's horror over who'd caught them. The expression McKenna wore was one of cold indifference but her eyes...

Kurt waved his card in front of the keypad, disengaging the lock. Patrick disappeared inside without a backward glance.

"It wasn't what it looked like."

He couldn't count high enough to describe the number of times he'd heard that lame-ass line. Never once had it passed his lips before now. Even he wanted to roll his eyes. Seriously? He couldn't think of anything better? It was cold enough that Kurt could see his breath. McKenna wasn't wearing a coat. Her bare arms bugged him. It made her seem all the more vulnerable.

"It's one thing to be stupid and a whole other to know it. Either way, I'm not enjoying it. Turns out, Gray was right all along."

He didn't understand anything she was saying. Not that she intended to give him time to decipher her words, it seemed. He was staring at the empty space where she'd been standing a full five seconds after she walked away.

*

It had taken McKenna twenty minutes to decide she wouldn't get a single word written after Kurt left. The look on his face when she'd refused to go with him kept intruding. He'd seemed so unhappy. Damn, she was such an idiot. All the times Gray accused her of secretly wishing for a bad boy while promising that type would only hurt her came crashing back. It hadn't been true then and it wasn't the truth now. She didn't want a bad boy. She'd craved Kurt.

"Hold up. McKenna, don't leave it like this. Talk to me. Please?"

McKenna's heart twisted. Why couldn't he let her go? It wasn't as if he cared about her in any way. At the door of her Camry, she spun and unleashed her fury. "What, Kurt? What do you want to hear?"

He looked desperate. She'd fallen for it too many times already. "I want you to say you believe I didn't instigate anything. He came on to me."

A wry smile pulled at her lips. She was incapable of holding it back. "But I don't. Believe you, that is," she admitted. "From the moment we met, I knew I was being fed bullshit at every turn. I told myself it didn't matter. You're sexy as sin. I'd be okay if you weren't really interested in keeping me. You're amazing in every way. I could live with only having part of you. What could it hurt, right?" A derisive snort escaped her. "The thing is, out of the two of us, I'm the bigger liar. Turns out, it does matter. I do want all of you and this does hurt. A lot." If he responded, she didn't hear it. Her mind turned inward. Memories suffocated her. "I guess I had this coming. Karma is a patient bitch, it seems."

McKenna's eyes focused on Kurt. Her brain refused. She could see his mouth moving but not a hint of sound reached her ears. Even though he was trying to talk to her, she got into the car, closing the door on his words. She'd survive this the way she did everything, by shutting down.

Chapter Five

How the man didn't feel McKenna's stare prickling at his skin was beyond her. It took her a good ten minutes to decide he was indeed the same man from the match against Kurt. His size and muscular jawline were unique but she didn't take it as a given. Considering Vegas' high population, there was every probability there could be more than one man with his build. It wasn't until something outside the window caught his eye and he turned to look that she became certain. The muscles in his jaw flexed. He'd worn the same expression that night.

"May I join you?"

He didn't seem surprised by her request. More than likely, he had strange women approach him on a daily basis. He eyed her for a moment before responding.

"Have we met? You look familiar."

Unsure of what the odds were of him remembering her from the Warehouse District, she weighed her words before deciding on the truth. "I was with Kurt the night you were injured." She motioned toward his arm before realizing how ridiculous the move had been. It wasn't as if he didn't know which part of him had been damaged.

He waved for her to have a seat. He waited until she settled before asking any more questions.

"How did you find me?"

His inquiry confused her. "Are you in the witness protection program?"

The hint of a smile touched his lips. "No."

"Then your question is irrational." She flashed a grin to take the sting out of her words. "As it happens, I was sitting over there when you walked in." She pointed at the booth where her laptop still sat.

He didn't look. "I didn't notice."

"People usually don't."

"I find that hard to believe."

"I'm certain I am the expert in this case."

He didn't argue again. "You've been crying."

"I don't sleep." It wasn't a lie. She didn't sleep but she wouldn't admit to shedding a single tear. Tears meant she cared for the state of her heart. She did not. It had died with Gray.

"Miss Jones." Asher's voice broke into their conversation, saving her from responding. He wore a friendly smile. Even broken, her inner girl sighed.

She responded without thought. "It's Ms. Richards, actually. Jones is my

157

pen name."

"Ms. Richards, then. It's nice to see you again."

"You as well. Of course, I'm always happy to see someone who smells as good as you. It brightens my day." She added a wink to let him know she was playing. It was also an attempt to hide her surprise. He remembered her name. Of course, she remembered his too but she—unfortunately—never forgot anything. Sliding out of the booth, she motioned for Asher to take her seat. "I'll leave the two of you alone. Maybe say hi next time you're in," she said, directing her final words at Brian. He tilted his head to the side assessing her but she didn't wait for his response. Trailing away, she wondered if he'd bother or why she had.

All of ten minutes passed when a flower appeared at her elbow. She flashed

Christy a grateful smile for handling its delivery before absently reading the card. "Some people believe tulips are a common flower, forgetting how many travelers flock to Holland to see them in full bloom. You are a tulip. Even as many adore you, you're an overlooked treasure. As it happens, I find tulips fascinating."

McKenna thought tulips were a bit bland. She loved this one. "Ms. Richards."

McKenna glanced up to find Brian hovering at the edge of her table. "It's McKenna."

He bit down on his bottom lip, obviously attempting to hide his amusement. "Do you meet anyone without correcting them?"

"Not if they call me by the right name on the first try. Would you like to join me?" Accepting her offer, he settled his elbows on the table and leaned forward. Someone had raised him to look people in the eye, she surmised. It was a strong quality. She closed her laptop, showing him the same courtesy.

"So, McKenna Richards with the pen name Jones, are you the owner of this establishment?"

"Do you intend to file a complaint?"

A dimple appeared at the corner of his mouth. "No, ma'am."

He possessed an entire arsenal of manners.

"Then yes, I am. How's the arm?"

He stretched out the limb and flexed his fingers. Her eyes locked on the way his muscles flexed. "It's still weak. I'm working on it."

"I've never seen as many professional fighters in my life as I have the past few months. My theory is someone planted a sexy bush in the parking lot of my store and yes, I did say that," she added before he could point it out.

Instead of poking fun at her terminology, he eyed her questioningly. "I don't know about a sexy bush but you are right across the street from No Rival."

"The name does sound familiar."

Brian snorted. "It should. It's the most famous MMA training center in the United States. Even if you don't follow the sport, you'd be hard-pressed to miss ever hearing about it, since it's owned by the US heavyweight champion. They've also helped produce some of the world's top fighters. You've probably been tripping over them on a daily basis for years."

"Interesting," McKenna mused. His maroon t-shirt strained against the muscles in his arms and chest, complementing his mocha skin. Why were

161

women weak? "I've noticed there are several regular customers who possess more than their fair share of perfectly symmetrical features." It was the politest way she could think of describing the panty dampening muscular men who walked through the door each day. They gave her inspiration to keep writing. He eyed her carefully. A slow grin spread across his face.

"Oh. Ha. You're fucking with me."

He was intelligent. She liked it. "Yes. I'm sorry. It's a habit I have a difficult time beating into submission. I'm aware of No Rival." Before he could comment, she asked, "Do you plan to sue Kurt?"

Her rapid change of topics didn't seem to faze him nor did he attempt to misunderstand. "Even if it were an option, I wouldn't. I chose to face-off against one of the most vicious fighters in Vegas. It was a calculated risk."

"Huh." McKenna wasn't sure what she'd wanted him to say. It's not as if she hoped for anything to happen to Kurt. On the other hand, if Asher wasn't meeting Brian for business then it sort of pissed her off. Rhys had been nice to her. He'd not once called her crazy even after she'd asked to sniff Asher's skin. Was everyone she met a cheat?

"Rhys would kill me. Not to mention, Asher loves him." Was he a mind reader? "I didn't say a word."

"Actually, you did."

Fuck.

"Heard that too."

McKenna closed her eyes in horror. "I swear I'm not crazy. That's a lie," she amended immediately.

Brian released a low chuckle. It set her at ease faster than any words could have. "Why the pen name?"

"So the perverts who send me videos of themselves masturbating won't show up at my door."

He didn't miss a beat. "I hate it when that happens. Why were you crying?"

"I caught Kurt with someone else. I really don't sleep," she added in case he thought she'd been lying earlier.

"I don't either. Want to stay awake together?" A line appeared between his eyebrows. "I didn't intend to sound as if I'm asking you to have to sex. This conversation went differently inside my head."

"I didn't take it that way. I've been propositioned. It sounds more like this." She deepened her voice. "Hey baby you look tired. My face is real comfy. Why don't you have a seat."

A rumble of laughter came from

Brian's chest. He had gorgeous, white teeth and sweet, chocolate-colored eyes. Being in his company was peaceful. Her throat tightened without warning. The backs of her eyes stung with unshed tears. Brian's smile faded away.

"My mother passed away last week. Asher is, was her attorney."

"I'm sorry for your loss," she responded automatically, thankful for something else to think about than her problems.

"She'd been fighting a long time. It was almost a relief."

"No. It wasn't."

"No. It wasn't," he agreed with a bitter smile. "But it's what everyone expects me to say."

McKenna nodded. "When my husband died, the asinine comments were almost as hard to swallow as his death.

165

He's in a better place now. The mortician did a great job. He looks like he's sleeping. You have to be strong. It's what he would've wanted. Nobody knew Gray the way I did. That's not what he would've expected out of me. It was emotional blackmail to keep me from doing what I really wanted."

A wry smile twisted Brian's lips. "Scream? Rant? Break shit?"

"All of the above. You should do those things."

"I already have," he admitted. "Now, I want to forget, if only for a little while, or be someone else entirely."

It was the same as looking in a mirror for McKenna. "I'd be delighted to spend a night of no monkey-sex in your company. Do you drink?"

"Not often."

It was settled. "Awesome. You

should start. I'll drive."

Brian pushed his chair away from the table. "I'm in."

* * * * *

Sweat dripped from his face. It was a rare occasion but Kurt was about to lose. He could feel it in the air. His heart wasn't in it tonight and his opponent knew it. He swiped at his cheek. A flash of red told the real story. He was bleeding. The phantom smell of burning flesh assailed his senses. A roar began inside his head. Now wasn't the time for this shit. Another blow landed against his jawline. It snapped his head back. The room spun. He went down to one knee. Unwilling to give up, Kurt shot back to his feet. It caused the room to tilt on its axis. His back hit the mat. In the distance, as if through a tunnel, he could hear a bell chiming. Even as he was pulled to his feet and helped from the mat, everything seemed muted. Reality had lost its edge.

It wasn't until someone patted his shoulder Kurt realized he'd been staring at the locker across from his for longer than he cared to admit after getting dressed.

"Everyone loses one every now and again."

Kurt glanced over at the baldheaded guy who was attempting to reassure him. The man thought Kurt cared. Huh. Perhaps there were people out there who did. How much longer could he go on?

Baldy flashed him a conspiratorial smile. "I hear that guy whose arm you snapped is done for." He released a dry laugh, as if someone losing their dream was humorous. What an asshat. Who was this guy?

"They say he was good and even Rhys Collier expected him to eventually

168

take the title. Guess it won't be happening now." He chortled. The sound ran down Kurt's spine, snapping his last nerve. Without a thought, his fist snaked out. It landed in the center of Baldy's face. He went down and didn't get up. Kurt stepped over him, catching the shocked gaze of the only witness. He'd fought him once but couldn't remember his name. It was Josh or Greg. Something along those lines. One of those four letter names.

Kurt shrugged as he walked past on his way to the door. "He owes me money."

The other guy's blue Mohawk moved in time with his nod. "Gotta do what you gotta do."

Yep. If the men in this place understood one thing, it was paying in blood for a debt.

* * * * *

They were clinging to each other.

169

Otherwise, they both would've fallen down. Brian's arm seemed heavy across McKenna's shoulders. She squeezed his waist tighter, hard-pressed to say which of them held the other upright. Brian's drunken weight was enough to buckle her knees. Possibly, she should've suggested he quit drinking at least an hour ago. Hindsight and all that rot. Their laughter turned to silence as they navigated the lane behind G. Richards' Bookstore. Even though she hadn't consumed a drop of alcohol, she'd always had more fun watching other people let loose thanks to liquid fortification.

Brian waved his free arm in a wide arch. "It's in your throat." His random comment left McKenna confused. "What is?"

She felt him shrug. "Life," he answered as if it should've been obvious.

"If you think about all the times it has choked the air from your lungs, you'll picture it happening in your chest. That's not true at all. It's in your throat. I think that's why most people don't realize they're slowly dying. They think it's a panic attack. They're wrong. It's reality, squeezing the life out of you."

It was true. Her windpipe had been under death's squeeze since the moment she spotted Kurt with someone else. As the metal stairway came into view, McKenna's shoulders sagged in defeat. She didn't have the strength to face her apartment, her memories. Instead, she sat down on the bottom step. Brian followed her down. Shoulder-to-shoulder, they sat in companionable silence. Streetlights reflected off the brick walls. The wind rattled the chain-link fence separating the alley from the building next door. Each

171

breath they took transformed into white plumes hanging in the cold air. McKenna's mind had been in such a state of shock for so long now she'd moved past the ability to feel any external discomfort. Not to mention, Brian's large frame produced enough body heat that it was cozy at his side.

"I met my husband, Gray, in this exact spot." The confession surprised even her. She never talked about him, ever, to anyone. Brian seemed to be the exception to every rule. Once the first words fell from her lips, they kept coming. "My head was in the clouds, as always." She smiled to herself. She could still picture the day as if it happened that morning rather than years ago. "I walked right past him without noticing. Of course, I also didn't see the stairs either. I tripped. Gray snagged hold of me before I could hit the pavement." She chuckled. Brian held his silence and it helped her continue. "He ended up holding a handful of my breast in the process. I was so grateful, I might not have noticed if he hadn't been blushing. He was stuttering this crazy-long apology, but his eyes…. Wow. They told a different story." Her eyes fell closed as if she could shut out the memory of his heated gaze. It was impossible. "There was this wicked glint. I was captivated. God. I hate him sometimes for leaving me alone."

"How did he die?"

Brian's voice startled her. She'd almost forgotten he was there. McKenna made a helpless gesture before dropping her hands back to her lap. "A single self-inflicted gunshot wound to the head. That was the exact wording on the coroner's report." Brian didn't say a word to encourage or discourage her but she couldn't stop. She nodded toward the back parking lot. "It was right there. In his car so I wouldn't have to clean up the mess." Her throat tightened, thankfully cutting off any further admissions. She wanted to cry. There weren't any tears left. Brian hugged her to his side.

"Life is hard work. Of course, that's no excuse for him to leave you in such a way."

"It was my fault." It was the first time she'd said the words aloud. It hurt more than expected. "He was sick when we met. Stage three non-Hodgkin lymphoma," she explained. "He'd already begun chemo and lost his hair. I didn't care. There was this spark inside him. I couldn't stay away. He was so intelligent and quick-witted. I wanted to crawl under his skin to be closer to him. Even the knowledge he might not make it didn't stop me from jumping at the chance to marry him." Chill bumps rose as the phantom sensation of Gray's mouth against her skin rushed through her. "One night, I was sitting beside his hospital bed and I thought my mind would snap. There was this pad of paper and pen on the nightstand and I started writing. I couldn't stop. For the first time in a long time, I'd found an outlet for my rage. I was going to lose him and I couldn't stop it from happening. Gray hated it. He read every word, trying his damnedest to be supportive. Eventually, he resented it. He accused me of wanting someone different than the man I'd married." Bitterness welled inside McKenna. No matter how hard she tried, she couldn't forget the way he'd made her feel as if she needed to keep herself hidden. She'd learned to retreat behind a mask of indifference.

"Why did he think your writing meant you wanted someone else?"

She shrugged. "It was my devil. He's the main character in my books," she explained. A sardonic smile tugged at the corners of her mouth. "Gray killed himself to set me free and do you know what pisses me off the most? It was him," she said without giving him a chance to answer. "Gray is my devil. He just didn't see himself the way I did."

At the confession, the tears came. It was a sudden burst, slamming into her with surprising power. Sharing her past and Kurt's betrayal pooled with the extra surge of hormones in her system, making her cry harder than she had in a long time. In this, Brian turned out to be the same as any other man. Even through her tears, she could see the panicked look in his eyes. Reaching inside his jacket, he pulled out a handkerchief. For some reason, the sight of the square white cloth caused an unexpected gurgle of laughter to rise in her throat.

"Who the fuck carries a handkerchief anymore?"

Brian lifted one shoulder, holding the cloth out to her. "I guess I do."

A gust of wind whipped through the alley, mid-exchange, ripping the material from her fingers. It blew over the steel fencing.

"Holy shit." McKenna couldn't think of another way to express her surprise over how far it traveled. "And here you were trying to be all chivalrous."

Brian's face lit. "Never fear, milady. I can still save the day—er—night," he corrected as he shot to his feet. Running for the fence, he managed to scale it after several drunken attempts. The cold wind carried McKenna's giggles away when he retrieved the cloth with a victorious wave.

She clutched her chest. "My hero."

Even in the dimly lit alley, Brian's smile seemed luminous. Bracing one arm on the railing, he kicked a leg over. As if watching things happen in slow motion, McKenna swallowed down a cry. Brian's arm gave out and his inner thigh caught on the sharp edge of the metal links. A dark slash appeared before he had time to land in a heap on the ground.

Chapter Six

Staring blankly at the magazine on the counter, Kurt dropped his news without bothering to glance in Kerry's direction.

"You'll need to find a replacement to work the door at Affinity. This is my two-week notice."

She flipped the page on her book, seeming unconcerned. "That stinks but I'm not surprised. McKenna has to come first."

He barely stopped himself from rubbing his chest. The ache blooming there at hearing McKenna's name nearly crushed the air from his lungs. After a few minutes of silence, she finally closed her book. Setting it aside, she focused on him.

"Will I still see you around?"

"I don't see why not," he answered evasively. "Where do you train?"

Kurt kept his head down doing his best to pretend nonchalance. "What do you mean?"

Out of the corner of his eye, Kurt could see Kerry swiping at the air as if attempting to physically grasp for words. "You know, to fight. Where do you spar or lift weights? I know it's not here. You're not World Divisional so it's not No Rival. Are you on steroids? Do you go to the Y or have a home gym?"

"Sure." He wondered if she would choke him at his intentionally unhelpful response. Pausing for effect, he slowly flipped the page on his magazine. He wasn't sure why it was so much fun to fuck with Kerry but it was. When she didn't react, he glanced up. There was a crazed look in her eye. He bit back a chuckle.

Adding fuel to the fire, he kept his

countenance carefully blank. "What?"

There was a moment when he thought she might snap. The glass door separating the foyer from the gym swung open, saving his life. Knox strolled out. Nodding in his direction, he acknowledged Kurt before turning his attention on Kerry. Kurt wasn't offended. He preferred the loner lifestyle. The only exception to this was McKenna. He couldn't breathe again. In an attempt to stave off a panic attack, he concentrated on Knox and Kerry's conversation.

"Mandy wanted me to ask if you'd like to go to the hospital with us to see Brian tonight?"

"What happened to Brian?"

It was a toss-up as to who was more shocked by Kurt's interruption. Both Kerry and Knox seemed surprised he cared while Kurt mused over why he did.

Thankfully, Knox merely shrugged. "We're not a hundred percent certain yet. Rumor is he sliced open his femoral artery. Since his mom passed away last week, he doesn't have any family left and there isn't anyone we can call to get the exact details. One of the guys from Warehouse is a paramedic. He wasn't the one on the scene but was able to confirm it is the Brian Johnson we know. Once again, we're not family so the hospital wouldn't release any information to us. Luckily, Drew Alexander's wife, Aubree, works in the children's building. She was able to keep an eye on his condition. Seems he made it through surgery and is stable."

"I'm glad to hear he's okay. Do they know how it happened?"

Knox appeared hesitant as he answered. "No one knows for sure. There's a rumor it might've been intentional."

"Seriously? He doesn't seem the type." Of course, Kurt knew people usually didn't. It was always the ones people didn't suspect.

Knox shrugged as if his thoughts mimicked Kurt's. "Maybe we'll find something out tonight." Switching his gaze to Kerry, he asked. "What should I tell Mandy?"

"Sure. I'll go."

As they made plans to meet later, Kurt stewed. His temper always cost others. He hated the thought he might be responsible for ruining Brian's career and the man's mother had passed away. Grief was a funny thing. It could show up in the strangest of ways.

When they were once again alone, Kurt spoke without thinking. "Maybe I should go see him. I don't have anything going on today."

"Would it make you feel better about what happened?"

He hated when people tried to psychoanalyze him. "If I'd been carrying around any guilt, I would've gone to speak with the man before now. This isn't about what happened between us."

Kerry eyed him in such a way he wondered if he'd allowed her to see too much. He kept his expression clear of all emotion. She growled and he almost sighed in relief. There were parts of him he wouldn't share.

"In any case, maybe take McKenna with you to soften the beach, as they say."

He glanced back down at his magazine. There were issues he couldn't mask behind a blank stare. His heart breaking was one of those.

"Yeah. I don't know if that's such a good idea."

Kerry surprised him by groaning. "Damn. Sorry. I forgot about her husband's suicide. If Brian's injury was self-inflicted, it might be hard on her."

His brain ceased working before a thousand-piece puzzle snapped together inside his mind.

"I'll go alone." The absently spoken words came automatically while his mind replayed every detail of his time with McKenna. There had been hundreds of details about her life he'd wanted to know. Why hadn't he asked or dug harder when she resisted? But he knew. Forcing her to open up meant he'd have to do the same.

"What did you lose?"

"Everything."

Those words haunted him. Every second he spent alone since losing McKenna he'd spent replaying every cryptic thing she'd said.

"Karma's a patient bitch, it seems."

She drove him crazy. He almost snorted. It's not as if he had far to go. *"I assumed a place named G. Richards' would be owned by a G. Richards."*

"It was. He died. Now it's mine."

He had to get out of there. Slowly, in hopes of not drawing too much attention to his actions, Kurt backed away from the counter. He'd avoided too many facts for too long. It was time to find some answers.

"I'll let you know what I find out about Brian." His voice came out sounding steady If Kerry responded he didn't hear a word of it. In his head, he was already googling McKenna Richards.

* * * * *

Relaxing deeper into her chair at the edge of Brian's hospital bed, McKenna attempted to bury her feet beneath him. He lifted his uninjured leg. She flashed a

186

grateful smile at him over her notebook as he allowed her to burrow underneath his thigh. The moment she settled in place, he dropped his knee, lending her his warmth. Most people would bitch about her having her feet kicked up onto their bed. Brian wasn't like anyone else.

"It's damn cold in this place. I wonder what they have against heat."

"No shit," Brian agreed. "At ten grand a night, this is the worst hotel I've ever stayed in."

McKenna snorted. She tried her best to infuse a bit of humor into the sound. It wasn't easy. As hard as Brian tried to make it seem like he didn't care, she knew this was another expense he couldn't afford. A perfunctory knock landed on the door before it swung wide without waiting for permission. The same doctor who'd treated Brian the night before came sweeping in. His gaze was locked on the laptop in his hands. McKenna watched him, wondering how many hours a week he worked. He looked tired. She eyed his nametag. Dr. Harley Winthrop. For some reason, she found the name interesting. Winthrop sounded like a rich surname but Harley seemed an odd match. At around five-foot-seven he only stood around two inches taller than she did. She was also fairly certain she outweighed him by a good ten pounds. His hair stood on end and he wore a pair of those god-awful shoes that looked like a duck's feet. In spite of all those factors, he had nice eyes. They made her think he did care about his patients.

Glancing up, he caught her staring. He cleared his throat and switched his gaze to Brian before speaking.

"Well. It appears your body will

accept the blood transfusion. However, considering your size and the fact your movements will be a bit awkward due to the sprained ankle, I'm going to keep you another night. If you were to twist the wrong way too soon, you could reopen your wound and bleed out in a matter of minutes." Brian was nodding. McKenna could feel his frustration. "You were extremely lucky your..." He paused, motioning in her direction as if searching for a description or hoping they would provide one. "Friend," he said almost questioningly.

"McKenna," she supplied, intentionally being unhelpful.

He gave a sharp nod as if the matter was settled. "You're lucky your friend was there when your femoral artery opened. Even then, if she hadn't known exactly what to do, you'd be dead."

189

"The lower half of the male anatomy has always been my specialty."

Brian snorted. The doctor didn't so much as flinch at her comment. "Be that as it may, I would feel better with one more night of observation."

The more the man spoke the bleaker Brian's expression became.

"What if I promised to stay with him and ensure he doesn't do any further damage, could he go home today?"

A tiny smile hovered on the doctor's lips. "Considering your extensive knowledge of the lower half of the male anatomy, I'd be more inclined to think the odds were higher of him reopening his wounds due to strenuous activity with you there."

McKenna narrowed her eyes at him. "Oh. You're a naughty one." Switching her attention to Brian, she grinned. "I like him. You should look into keeping him after you leave here." If Brian was the least bit embarrassed by her behavior, he didn't show it.

"Hmm," the doctor said noncommittally before adding. "Ditto." Her eyebrows rose in surprise and he chuckled over her reaction. "I'll be back to check on you later...both of you," he tacked on.

McKenna's face heated. His laughter followed him from the room. The moment he disappeared, a sound escaped Brian, making her realize how hard he'd been trying to hold back his amusement. Since the doctor left the door standing open, he didn't let it fly the way he obviously wanted. Drawing an audible breath, he managed to keep it together. Humor lit his eyes.

"Have you ever met anyone who didn't find you irresistible?"

"Daily," she answered without hesitation. Dropping her gaze to her notebook, she clicked open her pen. "You'd be surprised by the sheer number of people who don't find me the least bit appealing."

"The world is filled with stupid people. You can't count those."

Brian was sweet. Nice people were few and far between. A picture of Gray floated across her mind. She hated that his face faded from her memory a little more every day. Already, the tiny details were gone.

"Do you need anything?" she asked, suddenly in need of air. "I could run by your place and grab you a change of clothes or get you some real food."

Brian shrugged. "If I had anyone else to ask, I would. You've already done enough for me but I also think you need a break from this place."

She handed him the notebook. "Write down your address and a list of what all you need." She refused to admit he was right. "Of course, I'll probably run home for a minute too. I need a shower."

"Take your time. I'm exhausted." He winked. "It's hard work keeping you company."

Even though she knew he was trying to make her feel better about taking off for a little bit, she still felt guilty for leaving him alone. "I'll hurry."

With an address and keys in hand, McKenna made sure Brian had everything he needed before heading out. He was already half-asleep from the pain medicine before she began quietly closing the door behind her. With her focus on her task, she stepped into the path of something solid and walked right into him. His scent surrounded her. Her body knew his. His hands clasped her waist, preventing her from moving away. The sensation of his heat against her skin demolished her already frayed nerves. Kurt didn't release her.

"Isn't this an interesting turn of events." The low growl of his voice was so close to her ear, she sucked in a breath. When his words penetrated the thick haze in her mind, her temper hit the roof. He had a lot of fucking nerve. "It didn't take you long."

Unadulterated fury rendered her speechless. McKenna opened her mouth, intent on something. Even she didn't know what it was but it wasn't good. There was a possibility she would've cursed his name, spit fire or bitten him. Perhaps she would've done all three if Dr. Winthrop hadn't saved Kurt's life.

"McKenna, is everything okay here?"

She eyed Kurt's scornful expression for a moment longer before tearing her gaze away. The moment she spotted the doctor, her respect grew for the man. In spite of the doctor's small stature, his face was hard. Kurt was one of the most intimidating men she'd ever met. It didn't seem to matter to Dr. Winthrop.

Slipping out of Kurt's hold, McKenna focused on her savior. "Yes. I'm fine." She added a fake smile to the lie. He didn't look away from Kurt. A silent warning passed between the two men, shocking her further. As far as McKenna was concerned, the doctor's bravery bordered on insane. "Did you need something?"

Shifting his laptop to one hand, he placed the other on the small of her back steering her away from Kurt's death stare. "I have a few follow-up instructions."

McKenna let him lead her away but she couldn't stop looking at Kurt's closed expression. She was still pissed-off. There was something in his eyes. She made it three feet. "McKenna." That's all it took for her feet to freeze to the floor. Even then, she couldn't speak. Fear and hurt choked her. A noise only a frustrated man could make came from the back of his throat. She half expected him to punch the wall. "I didn't mean it, okay?" He held her stare. "I know you better than that, okay?"

"Do you?" McKenna didn't wait for his answer. Turning her back to him, she walked away as fast as her feet would carry her. Thankfully, the doctor was able to keep up. When they reached the elevator and she was unable to avoid it any longer, she spoke up. "I'm sorry."

He didn't look at her. "There's no need to apologize. You had the situation under control." He finally glanced her way. There was a teasing glint in his eye. "Plus, I'm almost positive he wouldn't have killed me."

She wasn't. Of course, she had no intention of saying as much. The moment the doors slid closed, sealing them inside the elevator, he turned her way. "I'd ask you to dinner but after my super-manly display of bravery, you'd be obligated to say yes. The whole evening would be uncomfortable as you basked in my awesomeness."

In spite of herself, McKenna snorted. "Let's not forget how I'd also feel indebted to go home with you afterward. You'd be wowed by my talent and end up proposing right away."

A luminous smile lit his face.

"Narrow miss there."

Clasping her hands behind her back, McKenna rocked back on her heels. "Yep. Narrow miss."

He shook his head. "It's no wonder that guy was ready to beat his chest. I imagine you could have someone addicted in no time."

Being as how she hadn't been able to hang on to Kurt, McKenna knew there had to be some argument she could make. Her brain hurt. "Yeah, well, you should see what I can do with a tube of ChapStick and time on my hands."

"Do you ever behave?"

Even though she didn't think Harley was being serious, McKenna still thought it over before responding. "No. Not really." She flashed him a wicked grin, giving power to her words. Inside she was falling apart. Kurt's touch still branded her skin.

Her heart was a mess. The temptation to press the button that would carry her back to him was almost more than she could stand. Keeping her hands clasped behind her back, McKenna's nails dug into her palms. It was as if she'd lost a limb. She hadn't meant to get attached but she couldn't bear the raw spot where he'd been ripped away. It made every loss she'd ever suffered seem larger. As the elevator doors opened, she concentrated on not leaping out.

"Maybe I can ask you to dinner at a later time, after the gratitude fades."

"Maybe so," she chirped, surprising even herself with how honest her response sounded. Harley chuckled as he headed in the opposite direction. McKenna kept her fake smile in place all the way to the parking lot. That's where she fell apart.

*

Kurt watched McKenna's retreat with a sick feeling of dread. His dumbass accusation had—most likely—been the last straw. She'd never give them another shot. It was almost as if he wasn't happy unless he set a match to everything good in the world. He didn't tear his eyes away from the elevator until the last hope the doors would reopen faded away. Instead, he focused on Brian's room. Why had she been here? As far as he knew, the pair had never met. There was no help for it. Since he'd fucked things up beyond repair with McKenna, he'd have to get all the answers from Brian.

Without knocking, he threw open the door with more force than necessary. Brian jumped, as if the sound pulled him from the edge of sleep. Kurt immediately felt like shit. Even the man's lips were pale. What had he really suspected had gone on inside Brian's hospital room? Damn. He was such an ass.

"Sorry. I didn't realize my own strength," Kurt lied blatantly. He winced as he realized how terrible his words sounded in light of the situation. "I meant the door," he added, digging deeper. He swiped a hand over his face, wondering why he was an idiot. Brian sighed. For some odd reason, the sound set Kurt at ease. He focused on the man he'd come there to see. Determination to do the right thing settled in the forefront of Kurt's brain. Squaring his shoulders and not bothering to wait on an invitation, Kurt moved to the chair next to the bed. The expression etched on Brian's face let him know he wasn't welcome. He couldn't let it deter him.

Kurt opened his mouth intent on inquiring on the man's health. "What the fuck was McKenna doing in here?"

His eyes fell closed. Had he really said that? Brian growled. The sound caused his eyes to snap back open.

"You know, you've got a lot of fucking nerve. She's worth ten of you. Yet, for some reason she lowered herself to be with you and you couldn't keep your dick in your pants."

Everything Brian said was the truth. It's not as if Kurt could deny it. It didn't matter. He was still pissed off. "I know she's too good for me. Hell, she's too damn good for anybody. McKenna deserves the whole fucking world. None of that explains what she was doing with you."

Brian didn't jump to alleviate his curiosity or to dampen his temper. He merely eyed Kurt as if he was an oddity. "Wow. If it weren't for the whole catching-you-with-somebody-else, I'd almost think you were in love with her."

Kurt was unsure if he was more pissed off by the fact Brian knew so much about their relationship or if his fury over the man's words was a remnant of seeing McKenna leaving his room. Perhaps it was only his frustration driving him insane. He'd never been good at being helpless. Control was the only strength he had left to him.

"I do love her," he said, stressing every word. For some reason he couldn't explain, he needed Brian to know McKenna meant everything to him. If this man planned to steal the most important thing from him, he would damn well understand what it was he was taking away.

Brian had gone back to staring at him as if working out a puzzle in his mind.

After a moment, he shook his head. "I can't believe I'm saying this but I think you're telling me the truth."

Thank fuck. It was about time someone listened to him. He gestured helplessly. "Finally!"

"It doesn't change the fact you cheated on her." He didn't give Kurt time to respond. "Why are you even here?"

"I was worried about you," he answered. "I don't know why I bothered. There was a rumor going around that you tried to kill yourself. I realize now how ridiculous that notion is. All it takes is one look at you to see how furious you are with life. Angry people want to fight, not die."

Brian snorted. "Are you joking? Dude. Your ego knows no bounds. I get hurt during a fight with you and suddenly I'm so traumatized I'll kill myself? Not that it's any of your business but I got hurt

204

acting stupid. You're in love with McKenna, yet it's perfectly okay for you to still fuck whomever you want and what? Is she supposed to be so damn happy to have you she's not supposed to care?"

Brian's anger caught him off guard. Kurt wasn't sure how he'd gone from accusing McKenna of sleeping with Brian to being the one on trial. "It's not you, okay? I was casting my own weaknesses on you. Not to mention, I have all this guilt for not apologizing to you for what I did. I don't know why I'm explaining myself to you and I know you won't believe anything I say. As far as McKenna goes, I don't want anyone else. She's the only good thing that's happened to me in a long time. I'd never intentionally do anything to hurt her."

Brian almost seemed confused. For the first time, Kurt experienced a bit of hope someone might actually believe him. "I don't understand."

Kurt shook his head. "I'm not a good person. McKenna saw the backlash of one of my many bad decisions. I was attempting to disengage myself from an uncomfortable situation without hurting anyone's feelings when McKenna showed up." He didn't know why he was explaining himself. It wasn't as if it would change anything.

"From what I can tell McKenna is a reasonable person. Why didn't you tell her what you've told me? If things happened the way you say they did, then she's a smart lady and she would've forgiven you."

"I tried," Kurt said. Every ounce of frustration he'd felt since the moment she'd refused to listen to him came rushing back, showing itself in his words. "No matter what I said it was like she tuned me out."

Brian nodded, seeming to consider his words. His focus visibly turned inward as if processing everything Kurt said against everything he knew about McKenna. "I imagine that was Gray's doing," he said after a moment. Kurt couldn't believe how well Brian knew McKenna. He hadn't even known about Gray and here this man was psychoanalyzing the situation as if he'd known McKenna forever. He'd be damned if he'd allow Brian to know how little he knew about Gray.

"I can't imagine what he had to do with anything." Kurt wanted to pat himself on the back when his statement came out sounding as if he really knew what he was talking about.

It worked. Brian appeared to warm to the topic. "Well. He killed himself so he wouldn't be a burden to her any longer. He read all of her stories and believed she wanted some wild lifestyle she wasn't able to have with him due to his illness. To me, I'd think that sort of thing would fuck with your head. I mean, you'd question everything afterward, right? I imagine she believes if she wants something too badly, she'll destroy it. She probably searches for the cracks in everything. Wouldn't you think?"

Kurt was stunned. The final piece of the puzzle clicked into place in his mind. *Turns out, Gray was right all along.* Fuck. There were no words. "No. Gray was wrong."

Brian's brows drew together. Thankfully, he didn't question Kurt's craziness. "You should send her a text and be honest. That way she can't get away. Plus, it seems to me she values directness.

I think the harder you try to find a way around her the more she'll dig her heels in."

The picture of sunflowers that hung on the opposite wall held his focus as he turned Brian's suggestion over in his mind. As much as it chaffed to take advice from Brian, it wasn't a bad idea. Yep. He really needed to quit being a pussy.

* * * * *

McKenna almost made it out of the apartment before the knock landed on her door. She'd stopped by Brian's house first and, after stopping by her apartment for a quick shower, she almost felt ready to face another night of sitting by his bed. The usual deliveryman wasn't a surprise. What he held in his hands was. Once he had his tip and was on his way, she eyed the pink envelope with suspicion. It wasn't the flower she'd become accustomed to.

Slipping it open, she inspected the contents. There was a tiny packet of seeds and a note.

"You have to plant this one to find out what it is. Hint—it's yellow and represents new beginnings. I hate that you're ruining yours."

He knew about Kurt. The knowledge slammed into her hard enough to knock the air from her lungs. It had only been a matter of time but still. She wasn't ready. In a haze, she finished gathering her things. What did he think of her now?

Halfway to the hospital, McKenna found the car turning into the cemetery parking lot. She didn't intend to go there. It was as if she couldn't stop it from happening. Even after finding a parking space and following the familiar path to Gray's grave, she didn't understand why she'd chosen to go there. She sat down, crossing her legs. Leaning forward, she set her forehead against his headstone right where they'd carved his name. He had been her best friend. The knowledge he'd never be there again was an empty space nothing could fill.

"There's no fairness in the world," she whispered, knowing wherever he was now, he would hear her. "You left me nothing but your ghost and insecurities. I'm so mad at you." She traced his name with the tip of her finger.

"I see you're still torturing yourself." McKenna's head whipped around at the sound of the man's voice. "I'd hoped with all the rumors swirling around about you dating Kurt, it meant you'd found some peace."

Gray's brother, Terry, sat on the bench behind her. Judging by the way his hands were buried in the pockets of his black pea coat, and the slight flush on his cheeks, he'd been there awhile. She wanted to growl. Life was all about kicking her while she was down. She'd managed to avoid Terry since Gray's death. It seemed today wasn't meant to be her day.

When she didn't respond, he added. "I knew I'd run into you here eventually. You've been avoiding my calls and letters."

Even though he hadn't questioned her, she felt the need to explain. She shrugged. "If I could trade places with him, I would. I can't. Hearing you say you hate me won't change anything." Except it would break her heart and that was more than she could handle.

"I figured as much," he said, more to himself. His expressionless face didn't make his statement any clearer. Awkwardly, she moved to stand. In a flash, Terry was at her side, helping her to her feet. With one of her hands clasped in his, he brushed away the dirt clinging to the seat of her pants with the other. Coming from anyone else, the move would've seemed odd but it was Terry. Everything he did was gentlemanly. She kept her gaze locked on his face. Her heart squeezed. Up close, she could see the dark circles beneath his eyes. He also looked so much like Gray that it hurt to be near him.

"Thank you." She pushed the words past her rapidly swelling throat. His eyes snapped to hers.

"It's too cold for you to be out here without anything on your arms." At his words, her teeth began to chatter. Except, she didn't feel the temperature at all. "For the love of—" He broke off, tore his coat from his shoulders and set it over hers. His warmth enveloped her. "I swear. I've never met another person who needed a keeper the way you do. It drove Gray insane."

She felt moved to point out the obvious. "Everything I did drove Gray crazy."

Terry nodded and steered her toward the car. "It most likely kept him alive four years longer than he would've made it on his own."

"I doubt it. He'd probably still be alive if it wasn't for me."

"That's not true. He'd given up already when you literally fell into his life. You gave him someone to fight with and something to fight for." She noticed his Chevy truck parked behind her Camry. Picking up the pace, she made a beeline for it. This was one topic she couldn't deal with. Terry pulled her to stop, forcing her to face him. "McKenna. Gray wasn't going to get better."

"I would've taken care of him," she argued, not wanting to hear it. His face softened. "I know but he didn't want you to."

McKenna's chest hurt and her nose stung. She really didn't want to cry anymore.

"If I'd been a better wife, he would've stayed for me."

"No one could've been a better wife. Why can't you see the problem wasn't with you? He wanted to be more. Things were going to get so much worse and he couldn't handle it. It wasn't your failure. We get very few choices in life. This was his. You're doing him a disservice by living this half-life when he wanted you to have everything." An unexpected smile touched Terry's face. "Kurt is exactly the sort of crazy Gray would've chosen for you."

A snort escaped her. "I'm certain

Kurt is the opposite of what Gray would've wanted."

His expression turned calculating. "Tell me something. Where did you learn the things you write about?" Her face heated. She was never, ever embarrassed. She was now. This was her husband's brother. Terry chuckled. "I almost hate to say this but you need to hear it. I knew my brother for way longer. When he got sick, the wild lifestyle he loved was gone, until you." His face lit. "You didn't see a dying man. To you, he was simply a man. I don't think you've ever realized what that was like for him. Inside, he was still the same Gray he'd always been but his body was failing. Being powerless really sucks. Then you show up. He told me once that meeting you was the same as being reborn." He may as well have punched her in the gut. Terry's face turned serious again. "Was it fair? No. Life seldom is." Terry visibly swallowed, making McKenna realize how hard this conversation was for him. "You're all I have left of him, McKenna. Please stop shutting me out."

"You have his eyes." To her horror, her voice broke at the admission. She wanted to bite her tongue.

He drew back slightly, as if she'd slapped him. "I'm not trying to hurt you."

She knew he wasn't. "And I'm sorry for ever hurting you." Before he could reply, she flashed a wry smile. "Next time you call, I promise I'll answer."

Chuckling, he resumed walking. "I'll drive you home. You're too tired to be behind the wheel."

"I'm not going home. My friend Brian is waiting for me at the hospital. He doesn't have anyone else," she added when he didn't respond right away.

Terry released a loud sigh. "I'll make sure your car makes it to the hospital for you so you'll have a way home later. Better yet, you can call me when you're ready to leave and I'll take you home. Is this why you have dark circles under your eyes?"

She nodded as she opened the passenger-side door of her car. "Yeah. He almost bled to death but I managed to get it under control." Gathering Brian's things, she made sure all the doors were locked before adding, "Hospital chairs haven't improved any since the last time I slept in one."

"I imagine not."

Terry opened the truck door for her. Pausing with one foot inside and one still on the ground, McKenna stared at Terry for a moment. His familiar calm demeanor remained in place. She felt like an idiot for forcing him out of her life. Time had healed a few issues but not all. It had also left him with a hardened edge she didn't remember. Terry's hair had a hint of red to it. Gray had always claimed he had the temperament to match but McKenna had never witnessed it. On the other hand, his mind was every bit as sharp as Gray's had been. She knew exactly what she was up against there.

"What time did I leave this hospital this morning?"

His mouth turned up at one corner. "Get in the truck, McKenna. You have my coat and it's freezing out here. You can tell me on the way to the hospital why you're determined Kurt cheated on you and how you ended up behind G. Richards with Brian Johnson last night."

She'd thought as much. Swinging her foot inside, she allowed him to close the door. No doubt, he knew more about

219

Brian's injuries than she did. Thankfully, Terry pulled away from the curb without demanding answers. Her phone chimed, alerting her to an incoming text and she dug around until she found the phone. An irrational fear something had happened to Brian while she'd been gone ran down her spine. When she spotted Kurt's name on the face of her phone, she almost deleted the message without reading it. In the end, she couldn't resist the temptation. He was the one object she couldn't seem to go completely without.

"It occurs to me, I can remember the first lie I told you. It turns out, I'm indeed stalking you. If you won't ever speak to me again, please let me say this much. I was scared to let you see all of me because I didn't want to lose you but I guess it's too late now. Even though you won't believe me, it doesn't change the facts. I love you.

There was never any real hope you'd feel the same but still."

McKenna pressed the phone to her stomach as if Kurt could somehow feel her holding him. Her heart raced. The temptation to text him back caused her palms to itch. It was insane the way he made her want to forgive him any transgression as long as she could touch him. Staring out the passenger-side window, she kept her gaze locked on the passing businesses. It made it easier for McKenna to speak when she pretended she was alone. She'd always been good at talking to herself. Of course, Terry's silence helped as well.

"I had this dream last night. When I woke up, I realized how my brain had broken down my life completely. There was this buffet and I was at the front of the line. When I got my drink, it had this tiny straw in it. It wasn't long enough for me to use. It didn't seem to matter. I still left it in the cup. The drink came out in three different flavors. Of course, that wasn't what I wanted but I shrugged, thinking maybe I'd like it. I'm not scared of new things." She shrugged, mimicking the images in her mind. "The moment I reached for a plate, the guy setting out the food pulled the tray of dinnerware away. Again, I laughed and shook my head, patiently waiting for him to set out a new batch. This whole time, I never lost my good humor. People were going around me in line as if I wasn't standing there. I was accepting. There was this smile on my face as if I didn't expect more because that's the way things are for me. I have to work twice as hard to get to the same spot other people seem to reach with half the effort. Happiness lasts half as long for me. The moment my eyes opened this morning, I felt resigned." She motioned, helpless, with her free hand. "It's not as if I can act like the dream was some crazy, random shit. It was dead-on. If I'm happy, I expect it to end at any moment. If something truly wonderful happens to me then I brace myself for whatever horrible event is waiting around the corner for me."

"I don't believe in karma or a balanced universe. Whatever it's called."

McKenna jumped in surprise at the sound of Terry's voice. He'd been so quiet she'd not expected him to comment at all. Her gaze shot to him. She was intrigued. As far as McKenna could remember, she'd never heard anyone openly admit to not believing in cosmic balance.

"You don't?"

He shook his head. "I suppose I did at some point in my life. Of course, back then I didn't realize how many bad people seem to have all the luck while the best people I know get nothing but life's boot heel. On the other hand, I do think if you're a genuinely good person then other people will flock to you. Their support will offset the bad." Glancing away from the road for a second, Terry flashed a wry smile, adding, "If you let them."

In light of his confession, she found herself making one as well, before she could lose her courage. "I'm pregnant. That's how I knew it was inevitable I'd lose Kurt."

Terry's reaction was almost funny. It eased some of her guilt over her complete lack of memory when it came to taking her birth control pills. Oops. His head whipped around. Their gazes collided. The car slowed to almost a stop, as he seemed to forget he was driving. The blaring of a car horn forced his focus back to the road.

"Um. Well." He cleared his throat. She wanted to chuckle until he startled her by exploding. "You fucking knew you were pregnant and you were still sitting outside on the cold ground without a coat. What the fuck is wrong with you?" She didn't think he expected an answer. Proving her thoughts correct, he continued his rant. "You were out saving some guy's life and sleeping all night in a chair at the hospital. Goddamn it. You should be taking care of yourself." A hint of irritation wormed its way under her skin at the insinuation she didn't take care of herself. She'd been alone a long time without help and survived. His next words wiped away any hint of aggravation she'd worked up. "My brother might be gone but I'll never stop thinking of you as my sister.

That's my goddamn niece or nephew you're risking."

Her eyes and nose stung with unshed tears. Terry was furious. It was obvious in the flush of his cheeks and the way his nostrils flared. She'd never been happier to incur someone's wrath. Reaching across the space between them, McKenna brushed her knuckles along the line of his jaw.

"I love you too, Terry."

* * * * *

The odd expression on Terry wore matched the one on Brian's face. She almost smacked herself across the forehead. She'd assumed the men had met before. It was obvious they had not. Here she'd brought a stranger into Brian's hospital room. They were eyeing each other.

"Oh my gosh. I'm so sorry. I

assumed the two of you had met before because of No Rival."

"I gave up my membership when I lost the title," Terry said, interrupting her.

She might have known it if she'd stayed in touch. He didn't appear to have lost his edge or be out of shape. After giving herself an internal lecture, she made the introductions. "Brian Johnson, this is Terry Richards. He's my brother-in-law. He gave me a ride." She waved in Terry's direction as if she could possibly be referring to anyone else. Motioning in Brian's direction, she added. "Terry, this is Brian. He's my friend."

"I've heard of you, of course but it's nice to meet you in person," Brian said.

Terry's light green eyes took on an odd glint at Brian's words. McKenna was fascinated by the change in him. She'd never seen him be anything other than the proper gentleman. He didn't return the pleasantries. In fact, his tone bordered on rude when he finally responded. "Do you intend to return to the cage?"

McKenna removed his coat. Handing it over, she hoped he'd take the hint and leave. As he slipped it over his shoulders, her gaze moved to Brian. She was hard-pressed to say whether she was more surprised by Terry's sharp tone or Brian's expression. He seemed more confused than offended. His eyes followed Terry's motions as he straightened his jacket.

"I'd like to," he finally answered. "Unfortunately, I'm not sure I'll ever regain the strength needed to truly compete."

Reaching inside his jacket, Terry came out with a business card. "You should call me sometime. Maybe I can help you get back into fighting shape."

Brian accepted the card. He didn't look at it as he set it aside.

"Maybe so."

McKenna could tell from his tone, Brian didn't have any intentions of taking Terry up on his offer. It was obvious Terry knew it as well. His smile turned bland. "I'll leave you to your rest." Terry's eyes still held a hint of something McKenna couldn't decipher. He nodded in her direction before showing himself out.

"You should take Terry up on his offer."

Brian looked uncomfortable with the topic. He brushed his hand over the back of his neck. "Yeah. I don't know, McKenna."

"He's one of the best," she cajoled. "He could help."

Brian blew out a sigh. "That's the problem. It's one thing to look like an idiot in front of people who aren't any further along in their career than I am. It's a whole other experience to do it in front of a former champion and a stranger. It's just..."

"Yeah. I understand. Really though, I look like a fool twenty-four hours a day. You could handle it for a few hours a week if it meant reclaiming your dreams."

"You should take your own advice," Brian grumbled, leaving McKenna to puzzle over his meaning.

Chapter Seven

Sled hockey had always been one of those things Kurt found inspiring. Since his return from Afghanistan, he'd intentionally surrounded himself with things that made him feel good. Music soothed him. Fighting offered him a release. Volunteering kept him insulated from hell. Watching amputees find a way to hang on to the things they'd loved to do before losing a limb gave him hope for humanity.

As the men pushed themselves across the ice on the sleds, tempers were every bit as high as they'd been when the men were on skates. By the third fight, Kurt blew his whistle.

"For fuck's sake guys. What's up with all of you today? Pull your shit together." Some general grumbling about this being a real man's sport rang throughout the group but things improved a bit by the third period.

"Are you going to Drew's Wounded Warrior Benefit Auction tonight?"

On top of being the US Champion and owner of No Rival, Drew Alexander was widely known for his over-the-top charitable events. Kurt blinked at Terry's question, unsure whether saying no would be enough. Perhaps this is one of the times "hell no" was more appropriate. Instead, he chose a more diplomatic approach.

"You know I don't fit in with that crowd."

"Yeah. Well, normally I'd let you get away with that excuse. In this case it won't fly. Would you like me to tell these guys you don't intend to go?"

Kurt let a colorful curse fly. Terry smirked. No doubt the man knew he had him. "There's one more thing," Terry added, making Kurt groan. One more thing was never good. He was right. "It's a black tie event."

"Fuck you," Kurt said, making sure he put every ounce of his irritation into the two words.

"So, I'll pick you up at eight?"

Kurt might have to resign himself to going but he didn't have to be happy about it. "Wonderful," he said in his driest tone. "You're the hottest date I've had all week."

"All week? I'm honored but I still won't put out on the first date."

"Great. A high-maintenance piece of ass. Just what I've always wanted."

Terry's eyes glinted in amusement. "Hey. Don't knock it. You'd never forget me." There was no mistaking Terry's tone. In spite of his best efforts, Kurt's eyebrows still hit his hairline. Now that he thought about it, he'd never seen Terry with anyone.

Kurt was as guilty as everyone else when it came to assumptions. In his case, he presumed everyone he met was straight until otherwise convinced. It seemed he'd been wrong in Terry's case.

"I'm almost tempted to try to make you eat those words but you know..." A low chuckle fell from Terry's lips. "You're not my type."

Pressing his hand to his chest, Kurt feigned heartbreak. "I'm everyone's type."

"Yeah. Yeah. Be ready to go by the time I get there. Drew has something up for auction I intend to win."

* * * * *

Terry hadn't been joking when it came to his intent to bid. The moment the auction began he abandoned Kurt to grab a chair as close to the stage as possible. Kurt lingered in the doorway without any real interest in the show. On the other hand, he was interested in McKenna. He hadn't known she would be there. The moment he spotted her, he hadn't been able to resist staring at her even as he kept his distance. Somehow, McKenna had managed to secure a seat close to the stage. She sat directly behind the three men in charge of running the event. Kurt suspected, Asher—who was sitting to her left with his arm draped over the back of her chair—had something to do with the matter. If Kurt didn't know the dude belonged to Rhys, he might've been jealous. Hell, he did know it and was still fighting the emotion back. McKenna was especially beautiful in her black dress. With her hair piled on her head, her gorgeous neck and a hint of cleavage taunted him. Every male eye in the room glanced her way, especially when she laughed. It was a captivating sound.

Positioning himself near the door, Kurt stayed out of the line of sight while keeping McKenna's every move in his. When he'd realized the items up for auction were the fighters from No Rival, he'd been concerned McKenna would end up taking one home. She'd held on to her silence with the exception of the occasional whisper in Asher's ear and encouraging him when the bids for Rhys reached a staggering amount. That is, until Brian went up for auction.

She didn't jump in right away. Instead, she waited until Terry made his first bid before throwing her paddle into the fray. Terry called out a number, daring McKenna with his eyes to top it. She laughed heartily while driving the price higher. Terry countered again with a ridiculous amount.

She audibly sighed, making everyone chuckle. "You're too rich for my blood. I guess I'll have to bow out."

"Sold!" The auctioneer's call brought a Cheshire cat grin to Terry's face. "Stealing a woman's date, what's the world coming to?" McKenna grumbled. Kurt found himself shifting positions in an attempt to catch her every word.

"I could've purchased him for you," Asher offered but she waved it away.

"I've never needed a man to keep me satisfied. One of my best talents is slaking my own needs."

All three of the men—who were sitting in front of her—swiveled in their seats at her comment. Kurt was torn between laughter and ripping off their heads. On one hand, the innocent look on McKenna's face was priceless. On the other, they were leering at his woman. She stared back at them. Her face devoid of all devilry. When—after a full minute—she still didn't show a hint of the naughtiness he knew her words had held, they finally turned back around.

A wicked smile touched McKenna's lips and he almost took a step closer to her. He knew in his heart she was about to show the world the reason he'd fallen in love with her. She winked at Asher. The gesture gave Kurt the strength to tear his gaze away from her face. Asher was visibly dying with suppressed laughter. His shoulders shook and he swiped at his eyes. She leaned closer to him but didn't lower her voice.

"There is this one guy, though. His name is Bob and when he's running on a full battery, he can do things. Whoa. He'd make a girl's head spin."

The men were back to staring at her in a heartbeat. Asher was staring at the floor, biting his lip until Kurt thought he'd draw blood. McKenna was still blinking innocently. She shrugged.

"Actually, it's possible one of you have met him before. He's in charge of whatever department helps out neglected wives. I believe his last name is Bullet or maybe it's Rabbit." She motioned as if truly searching for the name. "It's something like that."

They shook their heads, admitting they'd never heard of the man. Kurt couldn't believe they hadn't figured out she was screwing with them. The moment their backs turned once more, Kurt wondered if Asher would fall out of his seat from lack of oxygen. If there was an award for maintaining composure, he'd win it hands down. Asher switched between glancing at the ceiling and visibly gulping down air. The pair stood, heading for the dining area. Most of the tables had been removed, transforming it into an open bar for the evening. Halfway there, Brian and Rhys joined them. While Asher and Rhys broke away to go their separate ways, McKenna and Brian claimed the only open table at the edge of the room. Kurt went straight for the alcohol. Even though he knew he'd regret it later since it tended to make the nightmares worse, he needed a drink.

* * * * *

It seemed no sooner had McKenna slid into her seat than Brian nodded at someone across the room and was off again. He'd been adamant about her joining him for the event. She'd spent the majority of the night with everyone except him. Not that she cared. A tingle skittered across the back of McKenna's neck, as if someone was watching her. She turned her head and the crowd parted. He was there. Leaning against the bar, a tuxedo straining against his muscles, Kurt regarded her without an ounce of emotion on his face.

It was almost cruel God had made Kurt so beautiful. Gazes followed him everywhere he went. He made people want. McKenna knew from experience how physically painful it could be to long for something out of reach. Holding her stare, he touched his champagne flute to his lips. A flutter began in her stomach. She ached. As much as she wanted to look away, she couldn't. Her hands itched to touch him. It was unfair. She envied the glass. His mouth should be on her instead.

Even as he moved in her direction,

she was incapable of forcing herself to look away. He'd said he loved her. She hadn't misread his text. There wasn't a hint of it showing as he claimed the seat across from her. The powers of destruction he held were limitless.

"You're not wearing shoes."

"You said you love me."

He didn't as much as flinch. "They serve food here."

"As I recall, you fucked me in my kitchen. Food is served there, as well."

A wisp of a smile touched his features before disappearing. "That's different." In spite of herself, she was interested. "How so?"

"It's your home. There's no telling where these floors have been."

The realization his concern was for her and not the other patrons should've surprised her, except it was Kurt. He calculated his every move. The general public never factored into his designs. The person in his sights was who held his attention. She dropped her gaze to the table, unable to stand the pain of staring into his eyes a moment longer. He was so complicated it made her brain hurt.

Kurt let out a derisive snort. "I promise I'm not complicated in the least. Fucked in the head, maybe."

McKenna winced at the slip. No matter how hard she tried, she couldn't break the habit of talking to herself. "You're not crazy. Trust me," she added with a tiny wave toward herself. "I'm not right in the head. I can recognize it in others."

He snagged her hand before she could drop it back to her lap. In spite of everything, she couldn't pull away. His fingers brushed over her knuckles. God help her. She wanted his touch.

"I am empty without you." Holy shit. Had she really said that? His eyes fell closed. Fuck. She had. In for a penny. "The thing is, at least half the time you're not genuine. I don't know what to believe but I do know I'm tired. Your games are out of my league. I'm so fucking exhausted. I don't want to play." She swallowed down the bitterness rising in her throat. The knowledge this would be the last time he held her hand sat like a stone in her gut. "I can't listen to another lie pass your lips and know I only have part of you. Let me stay in my fantasyland. I'm safe there."

"My parents were killed by a suicide bomber while waiting to board a passenger train."

She'd been prepared for anything except his admission. She held her breath, hoping he'd continue. He didn't disappoint. "I was a year and half away from graduation from Stanford at the time. In my self-righteous fury over their deaths, I enlisted in the Marines." A mocking smile twisted his lips, fascinating her. "I was bent on changing the world, making all terrorists pay for my loss. It seemed to me the best way to get in on the real action was to ace every test and training activity the government threw my way. Turns out, I was right. It had me right up front seeing all the shit nobody tells you about."

He disappeared inside himself. McKenna watched it happen but was powerless to stop it. After a moment, he blinked. Clearing his throat, he snapped back from wherever he'd gone in his head. "Anyhow, I came home and everything was different. For a while, I tried to be normal. It was gone. Lots of shit later, I met you. Everything changed. It's crazy because you know how I obsess over stuff. This thing with you is no different. I've gone over every second I've spent with you in my mind. There has to be something setting you apart. I had to know what it is. Why do you make me want to live again when nobody else has?"

McKenna shook her head, at a loss. "There's nothing special about me."

"But there is," he argued. "Everything about you is unique. However, the one detail I can't resist above all others is that you love me."

Goddamn him. She did. It consumed her. She loved him more than books.

"I've done a lot of terrible things, McKenna. You're not one of them. I need you to believe I would never touch anyone else because you're the only good thing about me." He held her hand tighter as if he expected her to bolt. She was incapable. "If you'd ask almost anything else of me, I'd give it to you but I can't let you go."

A weight sat on her chest. It was so heavy she almost looked down to see what it was. For the first time, she saw everything behind Kurt's mask. He wasn't hiding from her. The words fell from her lips without her permission. "I'm pregnant." He let go of her hand. At the loss of physical contact, a wall slammed down between them. McKenna swore the temperature dropped in the room. Her stomach churned. Kurt became a stranger. Dropping her gaze to the table, McKenna swallowed down the pain the way she had her entire life. Maybe she didn't have much but she had her pride.

"Yeah. Um. I guess that's my cue."

Gathering her shoes and handbag,

she pushed her chair away from the table. He didn't try to stop her. Brian was leaning against the bar, deep in conversation with Terry. The moment he caught sight of her, he straightened. His concerned expression made her wonder what he saw on her face. He didn't say a word. With a nod at Terry, he fell into step beside her as she headed for the parking lot. She didn't make it. The moment she pushed open the club's door, he overcame her. McKenna's feet left the ground. A squeak left her lips in her surprise. Cradling her to his chest as he would a child, Kurt's stride never slowed. Every line of his face was hard and he wouldn't look at her. She was almost scared to speak. Sneaking a glance over his shoulder, she caught a glimpse of Brian's smiling face. Obviously, he intended to let Kurt kidnap her.

"You're not running away from me again." As if to punctuate his promise, he finally looked at her. His eyes flashed with an inner fire. "And you're sure as fuck not walking outside in these temperatures barefoot while carrying my child."

A hint of rebellion rose inside her. "I didn't say it was your baby." He growled. Actually growled. She could feel the vibration of the sound from his chest. "It is but I didn't say as much," she grumbled childishly. Shifting her weight, he freed one hand long enough to press the button on a keychain. Yellow lights flashed to their left and Kurt changed directions, heading toward them.

"What are you doing?"

"I didn't drive here," he explained. "We're taking Brian's car."

Brian's car? "Traitor," she muttered before saying louder, "How will he get home?" Kurt's gorgeous eyes met hers once more. She wasn't comforted. "You shouldn't be worried about anyone other than yourself at the moment."

In spite of everything, a shiver of excitement ran down her spine. There were times when she was weaker than others. This was one of those. It wasn't enough for Kurt to lay waste to her life one time. He was an addictive form of destruction. It wasn't until they were pulling into the parking lot of a nondescript red-brick building she'd never seen before that McKenna thought to question where they were going. The realization caused an uncomfortable knowledge to settle over her. She did trust Kurt. The moment he'd swept her into his arms she hadn't worried where they would go only that he would leave her again at the end of the journey. How very stupid she was.

"What is this place?"

Digging around in the backseat, Kurt found her coat. It had been warmer than usual earlier in the evening. Now there was a definite bite to the air. "Put this on." Kurt watched her until she did as he bade. "The shoes too," he added. With a sigh, she slipped her feet back inside the nightmare heels. When he seemed satisfied she was properly dressed, he stepped out of the car.

"This is where I go every day," he said over his shoulder as he went.

At his confession, McKenna threw open the door and scrambled from the car before he could reach her. Even though he held her hand all the way to the door, his face was still devoid of all emotion. She hated it. When he let himself inside the building, he went ahead of her. His large frame blocked the inside from view. In her curiosity, she tried peeking over his shoulder but he was too big. The lights were so bright in comparison to the dark night, it was almost blinding. She glanced up at them. A catcall rent the air, pulling her focus away from the ceiling.

Kurt stepped aside and the entire building seemed to fall silent. It was immediate, as if someone hit the mute button. It was a fitness center. Except, it wasn't like any training facility McKenna had ever seen before. There were several pieces of equipment she didn't recognize. It also didn't smell like sweat. Everyone inside, which consisted of all of four people, stood frozen as she stepped through the doorway. After an uncomfortable moment of silence, a man who'd obviously been beating up a punching bag spoke up.

"Are we finally getting to meet the illustrious McKenna?"

Snagging her hand, Kurt hauled her closer to his side. "You are." He switched his attention to her and McKenna's confusion grew. These people knew about her while she'd never heard as much as a whisper about them. "McKenna, this is Cameron." As he pointed toward the man who'd broken the awkward silence, the man stepped forward.

He held out his hand for her to shake. Even though he was covered in sweat, she didn't hesitate to accept it. "It's nice to finally meet the woman who managed to rope Kurt."

"You have awesome eyes." They were too. Cameron's brow furrowed, showing his confusion. "I'm sorry," she said, automatically. "It's a terrible habit of mine to say the first thing that pops in my head." If anything, her admission only appeared to confuse him more. She felt move to explain her observation. "One of your eyes is slightly bluer than the other. They're gorgeous."

His lips parted in surprise or perhaps he intended to respond. She'd never find out. Kurt tugged her away. "All right, McKenna. Reel in your inner flirt."

She scoffed. "I wasn't flirting. I was being honest."

"I know," he grumbled. "That's what makes it so bad."

Cameron cleared his throat still seeming bemused but he changed the subject. "Y'all are dressed awful nice."

McKenna released a girlie sigh. "Oh. You have a sexy Southern accent as well. Your eyes distracted me. Where are you from?"

Kurt swiped a hand over his face as

if exasperated by her. His smile told a different story so she ignored him. Thankfully, Cameron did too. "Athens, Georgia."

"You're a long way from home. How did you end up here?"

"I was stationed at Barstow before I was sent to Afghanistan. When they shipped me back like this," he said, pointing to the side of his face. "I decided to stay." He was missing two fingers on the same hand she'd shook. How odd. She hadn't even noticed. Once she did, she glanced around the room again, taking a closer note of her surroundings. Everyone there had some form of injury. The guy lifting weights was missing a leg. There was a different guy on the treadmill with a prosthetic leg and arm. It was a rehabilitation center, she realized with a hint of surprise. In light of Kurt's earlier confession, she shouldn't have been taken aback but she was.

"We just left Drew Alexander's charity auction event," she said absently as she met Cameron's gaze once more. "That's why we're dressed up," she explained. She didn't want him to think she'd forgotten his earlier observation. His mouth turned up in one corner. "I'm not sure I'll be welcomed back again next year."

Kurt groaned at her confession but Cameron didn't look away from her face. "I can't say I've ever met anyone who was tossed out of a charity event. I'd think they'd be happy to have anyone who was willing to give them money."

McKenna could feel a smile tugging at the corners of her mouth. "I'm not for everyone."

A wicked glint entered his eyes. "I

find that hard to believe."

Kurt groaned again. "For the love of all things holy, don't challenge her." A luminous grin lit Cameron's face as he switched his attention to Kurt.

"Damn and she writes erotica. You're a lucky man."

Heat exploded across McKenna's face, causing him to chuckle. These guys really did know way more about her than she did them.

"I'm downright undeserving," Kurt agreed.

McKenna spoke without thinking. "No one is unworthy of love."

Kurt's gaze shot to hers. He directed his words to Cameron without taking his eyes off her. "It's late and I'm sure McKenna is ready to get off her feet."

"Of course," Cameron said immediately. Kurt finally glanced his way.

"I wanted to introduce McKenna to you while we were on this side of town." Cameron eyed her. "I'm glad you did. Don't keep her hidden away for so long the next time."

Now that McKenna knew about this place, they couldn't keep her away. "I will definitely be back."

With another shake of his hand, McKenna tossed a wave over her shoulder as Kurt led her back outside. He seemed almost subdued. His thumb brushed over her knuckles as he held her hand. McKenna didn't think he was even aware of the motion. She was. Her entire being locked on the feel of his calloused hand.

After starting the car, he didn't move. Kurt stared at some point in the distance. It was as if he'd disappeared inside himself.

"I like Cameron," McKenna said

when she couldn't stand the silence any longer. Kurt still didn't look at her but he did seem to come back to reality.

"I didn't mean to hide from you." He nodded sharply as if deciding it was indeed the truth. She wanted to see his eyes but he kept them glued straight ahead. "There's so much ugliness in the world." A sad smile touched his face, making her heart squeeze. "Being with you is beautiful, untainted." He finally glanced her way. McKenna's mouth went dry. Emotions were near to bursting from him. She could see it in his gaze. "I wanted to keep you safe from the damaged side of me but not one single time did I intend to shut you out. But, you kept details from me too."

McKenna had no idea what he was talking about. The bewilderment must have shown on her face because he snorted. "I don't think you meant to either. You never said a word to me about Gray," he explained. Her confusion cleared. Every moment they spent together ran through her mind. She hadn't. It wasn't a purposeful move. Gray was a topic she didn't intentionally broach. She was such a fool.

"You're so damn smart," she said after a moment. "From the first time we met, you've known everything about me. I guess I assumed you knew about him too. It seems as if you know all there is to know about everything." She motioned helplessly. "You're easily the most intelligent person I've ever met. Sexiness drips from your pores. There's a thousand things about you that keep me unbalanced. I can't compete."

Kurt sighed. "For the last goddamned time, there is no one who compares to you. I would never touch anyone else."

"Not other people," McKenna said, frustrated. "You. I can't compete with you. I can't figure out your mind or second guess you. If you want to know something, ask." Holding her stare, Kurt slowly nodded. "Okay then. Do you believe me? About that night at Affinity," he clarified. "I love you and want you, but I need this."

She mulled it over. In the end, she couldn't hold on to her anger. "I trust you."

His triumph was almost tangible. His face remained impassive. "Do you love me?" Even though she wanted to laugh, she kept it hidden. Pretending to think it over, she cocked her head to one side, eyeing him. In an instant, he shut down. She could feel him withdrawing from her. She launched herself at him, capturing his mouth with hers. The breath left her lungs as his taste filled his mouth. The love she felt for him was choking her.

Her roots stung as Kurt tugged at her hair, ripping away from her mouth. His lips moved to the column of her throat. Every nerve ending in her body tingled at the sensation of his tongue stroking her skin. Clutching his hair, she held him in place.

"I do love you. So fucking much," she admitted. "I'm sorry, baby." He froze. His lips still clung to her skin. "I should've believed you," she added. Cupping his jaw, she leaned away to look him in the eyes. "The fear of losing you ate at me until it was like I made it happen. Please forgive me."

In an instant, her ass left the seat. She was in his arms and straddling his hips without any idea how it happened. Kurt looked outraged. "No. I made mistakes and it came back to haunt me. You don't apologize to me, ever. Do you understand me?"

Damn. He was beautiful. Shaggy strands of blond hair hung in his eyes. Every line of his face was hard. This man loved her. It was almost too much. An unexpected wave of emotion overcame her. "Can I keep you?"

The question came out in whisper. Kurt's features softened. His fingers brushed along her back. "You couldn't possibly own me any more than you already do."

"Do you promise to show me your handcuffs and let me do whatever I want to your body?"

A dimple appeared at the corner of his mouth before disappearing once more as if he was trying to hold it in. "I'm a little scared now. You're a bit of a pervert."

She wiggled her hips, making sure to remind him that only a few articles of clothing separated them. "And?"

His eyes seemed to slip out of focus. "And I love it."

"Oh good," she sighed as she leaned in, touching her lips to his. "I'll rock your world."

"You already have, baby. You already have."

Epilogue

McKenna stood with her back to him at the kitchen counter. Kurt's cock lengthened at the sight of her sexy ass peeking out at him from the edge of her short t-shirt. Wrapping his arms around her waist, he swiped his hand over her rounding belly, silently sending his love to their child. Some days he still couldn't believe his luck.

Kurt eyed the overflowing vase. McKenna did her best to stuff the violets inside with the other flowers. He nodded at it. "How long do you plan to let this go on?"

"As long as Terry continues sending them, I suppose."

His mind shuddered to a stop. "Do you mean to tell me you've known all along who's sending you gifts?"

McKenna pulled a face. It went far at telling him what she thought of his intelligence. "Of course I do. Otherwise, it would be creepy."

"Of course." Even he could hear the dry note to his words.

"Terry used to send letters every day after Gray died. I guess he finally decided I wouldn't read them and he started sending flowers instead. Since I didn't realize the first one was from him, I accepted the delivery. He had me. They haven't stopped coming."

"Wait. Did you say Terry?"

She nodded. "Yeah. Terry. My brother-in-law. Since the two of you came to the charity auction together, I assumed you knew as much."

He was an idiot. A smile tugged at the corners of his mouth. "That bastard." With any luck, one day soon Terry would get what was coming to him. It would be fun watching him fall. Lord knew, it was the best thing that had ever happened to Kurt.

The End

Keep an eye out for the next No Rival book, Unattainable.

Author Bio

Charity Parkerson is an award winning and multi-published author with several companies. Born with no filter from her brain to her mouth, she decided to take this odd quirk and insert it in her characters.

*2015 Readers' Favorite Award Winner
*Winner of 2, 2014 Readers' Favorite Awards
*2015 Passionate Plume Award Finalist
*2013 Readers' Favorite Award Winner
*2013 Reviewers' Choice Award Winner
*2012 ARRA Finalist for Favorite Paranormal Romance
*Five-time winner of The Mistress of the Darkpath

Connect with her online:

--Website: charityparkerson.com

--Facebook:

facebook.com/authorCharityParkerson

facebook.com/TheMenofSin

--Twitter: twitter.com/CharityParkerso

www.ingramcontent.com/pod-product-compliance
Lightning Source LLC
Chambersburg PA
CBHW060624260626
47161CB00008B/2799